Contents

Introduction

This book aims to provide easy-to-understand, practical help for the non-specialist class teacher for whom the 1999 revised, further reduced version of the National Curriculum Physical Education document provides little practical help or specific guidance. The 'Lesson Notes and NC Guidance' notes that accompany each lesson aim to help teachers with main teaching points; summarise the main emphases; and explain what pupils should be achieving to satisfy good practice in physical education, generally, and in NC terms. Programme of Study, Attainment Target and Learning across the National Curriculum elements are translated into easily understood objectives appropriate for each lesson.

Awareness of 'movement'

The teacher's knowledgeable observation of the class in action is the starting point for all improvement and development. Helpful comments and teaching points made to individuals and the whole class should always be based on what has been observed. A pattern to follow, when looking at the several elements of movement, is a helpful guide.

1 What actions and uses of body parts are taking place? Are the actions being performed quietly, neatly, wholeheartedly, correctly and safely, always aware of others?

2 What body shapes are being clearly shown while moving and while still? We always have a body shape and we want pupils to know that it contributes to the appearance and efficiency of movements. Poor, lazy, limp, sagging shapes look unattractive and mean the body is not working hard. Firm, clear shapes need effort and look good.

3 Where are the actions taking place? Stage one, under this heading, will almost certainly involve the teacher in stopping pupils all travelling round, after one another, in an anti-clockwise circle. Good sharing of space for easy, safe practice; working in different directions and at different levels; and contrasting the use of own floor space with whole room space, all enhance the appearance of the work.

4 How are they moving? Effort and speed, like shapes, are ever-present features within an action and their conscious application is a major contributor to better controlled, interesting, contrasting and better quality performance. How firm or gentle? How fast or slow? How soft or explosive? When a pupil consciously starts to contrast a lively, strong, upward leap with its slower, softer landing, the movement awareness training is starting to show results.

5 How well do they 'select and combine their skills, techniques and ideas and apply them accurately and appropriately', a main requirement within the National Curriculum? Assessment of the pupil's progress and achievement will be based on their ability to plan and link together a series of movements. The quality of the eventual created dance will be directly related to the quality of the teacher's powers of observation and comments based upon this observation. His or her enthusiastic demands for the highest possible standards – the best and neatest actions; well-controlled use of body parts; firm, poised body shapes; good use of space and thoughtful application of effort and speed – will all have been influenced by an awareness, through observation by the teacher, of what is happening and what needs to be improved.

The aims of Dance

Education has been defined as the 'structuring of experiences in such a way as to increase human capacity'. Dance aims to increase human capacity under the following headings.

1 *Physical development* We focus on body action to develop neat, well-controlled, versatile movement. We want our pupils to move well and look poised, graceful and confident. The vigorous actions performed in Dance also promote healthy physical development, improving strength, suppleness and stamina.

2 *Knowledge and understanding* Pupils learn and understand through the combination of physical activity (with its doing, feeling and experiencing of movement) and the mental processes of decision-making, as they plan, refine, adapt, evaluate and then plan again for improvement.

3 *Artistic and aesthetic appreciation* Gaining knowledge and understanding of the quality-enhancing elements of movement is a particular aim of Dance. Such understanding of quality, variety and contrast in the use of body action, shape, direction, size, speed and force is a major contributor to appreciation of good movement. We want our pupils to understand what is good about good movement.

4 *Creativity* It has been said that: 'If you have never created something, you have never experienced satisfaction.' Dance is a most satisfying activity, regularly challenging the pupil to plan and present something original. Opportunities abound for an observant, appreciative teacher to say: 'Thank you for your demonstration and your own, original way of doing the movements.'

5 *Expression and communication* In Dance we communicate through the movement expression of the feeling or the action. We use, for example, stamping feet to express anger; we

skip, punch the air or clap hands to show happiness; we swagger, head held high, to express self-assurance. Similarly, we create simple characters and stories by expressing them through movements associated with them. The old or young; rocket, machine or leaves; puppet, animal or circus clown, can all be expressed through their particular way of moving.

6 *Confidence and self-esteem* Particularly at primary school, a good physical education that increases skill and recognises and praises achievement, can enhance an individual's regard for him or herself, and help to improve confidence and self-esteem. Dance lessons are extremely visual and offer many opportunities for seeing improvement, success and creativity, and demonstrating these admirable achievements to others.

7 *Social development* Friendly, co-operative, social relationships are part of most junior school Dance lessons. Achievement, particularly in the 'dance climax' part of the lesson, is usually shared and enjoyed with a partner or a small group. Pupils also share space sensibly with others; take turns at working; demonstrate to and watch demonstrations by others; and make appreciative, helpful comments to demonstrators and partners.

8 *Enjoyment* Dance is fun and an interesting, sociable, enjoyable physical activity.

9 *Eventual choice of lifestyle* It is hoped that the teacher believes that enjoyable, sociable and physical activity, experienced regularly at school in Dance and Physical Education lessons generally, can have an influence on the pupils' eventual choice of lifestyle, long after they leave school.

Implications for Dance teaching

1 Lessons will all have one thing in common – near continuous and enjoyable, vigorous physical activity. Lessons should be 'scenes of busy activity with everyone found working, not waiting'.

2 To justify the 'education' part of Physical Education, there must be opportunities for pupils to plan ahead thoughtfully to make decisions about their actions. They will also be encouraged to reflect on, and make comments on their own and others' actions and use these simple judgements to improve.

3 Pupils need to be helped to understand and use variety, contrasts and quality to develop their work. 'What actions? What uses of body parts? What shapes?' are the earliest questions. 'Where are you moving? What directions and levels? On the spot or travelling?' are the next questions. 'How are you performing? Are your movements soft and gentle or firm and strong? Are you performing in almost slow motion or is your action explosive?' are questions associated with exciting, artistic, good quality work with aesthetic appeal.

4 While there will always be much direct teaching and use of demonstrations to develop the class repertoire, there will also be much challenging to create original work. 'Show me how you can link these actions with a change of speed at some point.'

5 There will be much questioning of the class about the main features of the way we move to represent feelings, and about the particular way that inanimate objects or different types of people move to guide us, to represent them through movement.

6 Pupils who work hard to achieve and improve should be recognised, praised and helped to feel good about themselves.

7 Partner work or small group work should be a feature of most Dance lessons with pupils being brought closer together in a common endeavour.

8 In addition to the perspiration and deep breathing which the vigorous physical activity inspires, there should often be smiling faces expressing enjoyment. When asked why they like something, a pupil's first answer is usually 'It's fun!'

9 Class discussion should conclude that regular physical activity is good for you. It makes you look and feel better. It's sociable and it helps to make you feel relaxed, calm and fit.

'The Government believes that two hours of physical activity a week, including the National Curriculum for physical education and extra-curricular activities, should be an aspiration for all schools. This applies through all key stages.'

Programme of Study

Pupils should be taught to:

a *create and perform dances using a range of movement patterns, including those from different times, places and cultures.*

b *respond to a range of stimuli and accompaniment.*

Attainment Target

Pupil should be able to demonstrate that they can:

a *link skills, techniques and ideas and apply them accurately and appropriately, showing precision, control and fluency.*

b *compare and comment on skills, techniques and ideas used in own and others' work, and use this understanding to improve their own performance by modifying and refining skillls and techniques.*

Main NC headings when considering progression and expectation

* *Planning* – provides the focus and the concentrated thinking necessary for an accurate performance. Where standards of planning are satisfactory, there is evidence of:

a *the ability to think ahead, visualising what you want to achieve,*

b *good decision making, selecting the most apropriate choices,*

c *a good understanding of what was asked for,*

d *an understanding of the elements of quality, variety and contrast,*

e *an unselfish willingness to listen to others' views and adapt.*

* *Performing and improving performance* – always the most important feature. We are fortunate that the visual nature of physical education enables pupils' achievement to be easily seen, shared and judged. Where standards in performing are satisfactory, there is evidence of:

a *successful, safe outcomes,*

b *neat, accurate, 'correct' performances,*

c *consistency, and the ability to repeat and remember,*

d *economy of effort and making everything look 'easy',*

e *adaptability, making sudden adjustments as required.*

* *Linking actions* – with pupils working harder for longer, which is a main aim for physical education teaching, pursuing near continuous, vigorous and enjoyable action, expressed ideally in deep breathing, perspiration and smiling faces.

* *Reflecting and evaluating* – important because they help both the performers and the observers with their further planning, preparation, adapting and improving. Where standards are satisfactory, there is evidence of:

a *recognition of key features;*

b *keen and accurate observation;*

c *awareness of accuracy of work;*

d *helpful suggestions for improvement;*

e *good self-evaluation and acting upon these reflections;*

f *pleasure, sensitive concern for another's feelings, and a good choice of words regarding another's work.*

Example of a checklist

CLASS: Year 5 LESSON: September THEME: Basic actions	WARM-UP	MOVEMENT SKILLS TRAINING	CREATED DANCE
Plan, improve and refine performance, and repeat with increasing control and accuracy		✔	✔
Plan solutions to tasks, linking skills and ideas with precision, control and fluency		✔	✔
Respond to range of stimuli through Dance, working safely, alone, and in groups	✔	✔	✔
Express feelings, moods, ideas, and create simple characters and narratives	✔		✔
Compose and control by varying shape, size, speed, direction and tension		✔	✔
Traditional dances from different times and places			
Make judgements on own and others' performance and use judgements to improve own work		✔	✔
Sustain energetic activity and understand what happens to the body during exercise	✔	✔	✔

Teaching with 'Pace'

Always high on the list of accolades for an excellent Dance lesson is the comment that 'It had excellent pace' and moved along, almost without stopping, from start to finish. Lesson pace is determined by the way that each of the several skills that make up the whole lesson is taught. A pattern for introducing, teaching and developing each of the several skills is helpful.

1 **Quickly into action** Using few words, explain the skill or task clearly and challenge the class to begin. 'Show me your best stepping, in time with the music. Begin!' This near-instant start is helped if the teacher works enthusiastically with them.

2 **Emphasise main teaching points, one at a time, while class are working** The class all need to be working quietly if the teacher is to be heard. 'Visit all parts of the room, sides, ends and corners as well as the middle.' . . . . 'Travel along straight lines, never following anyone.' (Primary school pupils will always travel round in a big anti-clockwise circle, all following one another, unless taught otherwise.)

3 **Identify and praise good work while the class is working** The teacher does not say 'Well done' without being specific and explaining what is considered to be praiseworthy. Comments are heard by all and remind the class of the key points. 'Well done, Emily. Your tip-toe stepping is lively and neat.' . . . . 'Tony, you keep finding good spaces to travel through. Well done.'

4 **Teach for individual improvement while the class is working** 'Gary, swing arms and legs with more determination, please.' . . . . 'Ann, use your eyes each time you change direction to see where the best space is.'

5 **Use a demonstration, briefly, to show good quality, variety, or a good example of what is expected and worth copying** 'Stop, please, and watch how Cara, Michael, James and Christine step out firmly with neat, quiet footwork, never following anyone.' . . . . 'Stop, everyone, and watch how Julie is mixing bent, straight and swinging leg actions for variety.'

6 **Very occasionally, to avoid using too much activity time, a short demonstration is followed by comments from observers** 'Half of the class will watch the other half. Look out for and tell me whose stepping is neat, lively and always well-spaced. Tell me if someone impresses you for another reason.' The class watch for about 12 seconds and three or four comments are listened to. For example, 'John is mixing tiny steps with big ones.' . . . . 'Mary is stepping with feet together, then with feet wide apart.' Halves are changed over and the process repeated.

7 **Thanks are given to all the performers and to those who made helpful, friendly comments** Further class practice takes place with reminders of the good things seen and commented on.

Assessment

The National Curriculum checklist for Dance teaching on page 9 enables the teacher and school to confirm that they are aware of and aiming to satisfy the statutory requirements. In other words, teaching is taking place along National Curriculum lines. The focus here is on the nature of the teaching and the opportunities being provided.

When the focus moves on to the individual pupil to try to identify the nature of his or her progress and achievement, we concentrate on the main requirement for Physical Education within the National Curriculum. That is, it should be a practical and educational, doing and thinking, performing and learning activity. Assessment is most succinctly achieved under four headings:

Planning   Performing/Improving   Performance
Linking actions   Reflecting/Evaluating

Planning that is thoughtful, well-organised and well-visualised is the basis for a successful performance. Where a pupil's standard of planning is satisfactory, there is evidence of a clear understanding of what is wanted; thinking ahead to 'see' the intended outcome; originality and variety; an unselfish consideration for others sharing the space; and a willingness to work hard to achieve and improve.

Performing and improving performance, and expressing the 'physical' within Physical Education, is the most important of the four headings. The visual nature of dance allows achievement, assessed in the finished piece of dance, to be seen and judgements to be made. Where performing standards are satisfactory, there is evidence of: accurate, controlled, neat work, consistently poised, versatile actions; whole-hearted, enthusiastic participation; and an impression of confident, almost effortless work.

Linking actions into sequences of almost non-stop action, using features of the lesson's development during the previous lessons, is the ultimate performance goal as pupils work harder for longer and demonstrate that they can remember and repeat their poised, flowing, well-controlled movements. Ideally, there will be smooth continuity with good variations in the use of space, shape and effort.

Reflecting and evaluating on what has been experienced, or seen and remembered, assists the performers and the observers with ideas for further planning and adapting to improve their performances. Where standards are good, pupils are able to recognise the different actions taking place; point out the main features; comment on the accuracy and success of the work; suggest ways in which the work might be improved; and self-evaluate and act on own or others' comments to improve.

Lesson Plan – 30 minutes

Theme:
Unselfish sharing of space; instant responses to instructions; neat, quiet, travelling actions.

WARM-UP ACTIVITIES - 5 minutes

1 Show me your best walking as you visit all parts of the room.

2 When I call 'Stop!', stop immediately . . . . stop! If you are near anyone or anything, take one step away into your own space.

3 This time, walk along in a straight line, never following anyone. Swing your arms and step out smartly.

4 Stop! Be still in your own space, quickly.

5 Now show me your very best, quietest, neatest running, still in a straight line, never following anyone. Go!

6 Stop! Once again, let me see you all in a good space, not near anyone or anything (e.g. piano, wall, gymnastic apparatus).

MOVEMENT SKILLS TRAINING - 15 minutes

1 Stand in your good space where you can all see me. Join with me in some of the actions we can do on the spot.

2 Step with a good lift forwards in knees and front of foot. Swing your arms, 1, 2, 3, 4. Swing and step, lift your foot.

3 Like a boxer now, patter with a quick running action with feet hardly leaving the floor. Your arms stay by your sides and there is no lifting of your body. Your head stays where it is.

4 Skip now, lifting your whole body with each 'step – push; step – push; step – lift', and swing your arms strongly.

5 Bounce very softly, with toes hardly leaving the floor. Show me a good knees stretch as you go up, and a good knees bend as you land. Stretch, bend; stretch, bend; push, land; up, down.

6 Well done. You did those actions on the spot very quietly and very neatly. Now try them on the move as you travel to the ends, corners, sides and across the middle of the room, never following anyone. Go! Walk . . . . quick patter . . . . skip . . . . bounce. Keep going!

7 When I call 'Stop!', stop immediately, and stand in your own big space . . . . stop!

8 Well done. That was an excellent stop and I like your spacing.

DANCE - Clever Feet - 10 minutes

1 Often, when we travel in the hall, we come to a busy place with lots of others in the way. If that happens, we can keep moving by performing on the spot until there is enough room to carry on.

2 Let's practise a 'Clever Feet' dance. Do each action four times on the spot, followed by eight times while travelling. Let's try hard and do all four each time – stepping, pattering, skipping, bouncing. Start on the spot, pretending it's crowded. Go! Step on the spot, 3, 4; patter, patter, quickly for 4; skip and skip and skip for 4; bounce gently. Now we travel; step and travel, off you go, 5, 6, 7, now patter; patter, 2, 3, 4, quickly, quickly, now we skip; and skip and skip and travel, 5, 6, 7, now bounce; bouncing, 2, 3, 4, low and quiet, and start again.

3 Stop! Well done. You all kept going in time with the bouncy music. Let's look at demonstrations by each half of the class. Those who are watching can help by clapping for the four- and eight-count parts of our dance.

LESSON NOTES AND NC GUIDANCE

Pupils should be taught to:

a *respond readily to instructions.* The lesson is full of direct teaching and specific instructions. The instructions to 'Stop!', 'Go!' and to join the eight different parts of the dance climax reveal the inattentive or badly behaved who are dealt with. The instant responders are praised. If they are also asked to demonstrate, their continued enthusiastic participation is assured.

b *be mindful of others.* Space awareness is practised in the warm-up, where the teacher tries to prevent the typical anti-clockwise travelling round the room, common in primary schools. The instruction 'Stop! Be still and in your own space, quickly', makes pupils conscious of giving others good space to work in, as well as giving them an exercise in responding quickly.

c *recognise the safety risks of wearing inappropriate clothing, footwear and jewellery.* This, the first lesson with a new class, is the right time to establish the necessary traditions for the way they will always dress (and behave and respond) in their future Physical Education lessons. No watches, rings, necklaces; no long trousers that catch heels; no unbunched hair that impedes vision; no socks without shoes. Barefoot work is recommended because it is quiet, enhances the appearance of the work and enables the little used muscles of the feet and ankles to develop as they grip, balance, propel and receive the body weight.

Lesson Plan – 30 minutes

Theme:
Body parts awareness, particularly feet and hands.

WARM-UP ACTIVITIES - 5 minutes

1 Stand in your good space and clap hands to the music with its sets of eight beats. Clap, 2, 3, 4, 5, 6, 7, again.

2 This time, on counts seven and eight, smile and do a little, friendly wave to someone standing near you. 1, 2, 3, 4, 5, 6, friendly wave; 1, 2, 3, 4, 5, 6, smile and wave.

3 Still clapping, smiling and waving, walk round this friendly hall, meeting and greeting lots of others. Walk, 2, 3, 4, 5, 6, smile and wave; 1, 2, 3, 4, 5, 6, hello, hello.

4 Run or skip or bounce, in and out of one another. Do not clap, but still look at and recognise someone near you on counts seven and eight. You might do counts seven and eight on the spot, like we practised in the last lesson. I will be looking at your neat, quiet actions.

MOVEMENT SKILLS TRAINING - 15 minutes

1 Let's give our legs a little rest while you show me some of the actions that our hands can do. Stretch . . . . bend . . . . shake . . . . circle . . . . click . . . . clap, of course . . . . come together, then come apart . . . . point . . . . slap and make sounds on the body.

2 Try some of these actions in different places, above head, to one side, to front, to rear.

3 Make hand sounds on different parts of your body and mix them with the sounds of clapping and clicking. Let me hear your steady rhythm. 1, 2, 3, 4; sound and sound and sound for 4.

4 Good. Can you join together three or four different hand actions? Keep a nice rhythm, 1, 2, 3, 4.

5 Change now to practising three or four travelling actions with your feet and legs. You can repeat the steps, bounces, skips and even the pattering of our previous lesson – or use other favourites of your own, e.g. hopscotch, glide, slide, leap, chasse. (Chasse is a step to the right with right foot, closing left foot to the right. Side, close; side, close.) Repeat each action eight times and let me see you using your eyes to look for good spaces. Ready? Begin.

1 Find a partner and number yourselves, one and two. Number one, go first and show each other your three- or four-part pattern of hand actions. Repeat each action four times.

2 Do it again so that your partner can remember it.

3 Now, with number two going first, show each other your three- or four-part pattern of travelling actions. Do your pattern two or three times to help your partner remember it.

4 Decide whose travelling actions will be used. The other's hand actions will be used. The music is playing for you to practise. Each time, the leader may quietly say the actions, as a reminder. Practise now, on the spot, then travelling.

5 Sit down at this end to look at three couples who are working well as partners. Tell me what you like about their hand actions and the way they travel together.

LESSON NOTES AND NC GUIDANCE

Pupils should be taught to:

a be physically active. First and foremost, we want Physical Education lessons to be 'scenes of busy activity', with everyone working and no-one waiting. We also want our classes to enjoy the lessons and to understand that near non-stop activity, learning lots of interesting and challenging activities, provides such enjoyment.

Brief, easily understood instructions that inspire quick responses; lots of individual teaching and praise while the actions are happening; and an enthusiastic teacher who joins in as an example, are all contributors to a lesson's good pace.

b respond readily (and wholeheartedly) to instructions. We need to train pupils to respond immediately to fill as much of the lesson with activity as possible. We also want them to be wholehearted, putting everything into their work as they use joints to their limits; make shapes full and firm with no lazy sagging; and work hard to move neatly and quietly, under control.

Lesson Plan – 30 minutes

Theme:
Awareness of basic actions and contrasting body shapes.

WARM-UP ACTIVITIES - 5 minutes

1 With feet apart, reach up high with arms wide. Feel the strong, wide stretch right up to your finger tips.

2 Bring one foot in beside the other and bend right down until your back, knees and ankles are bent.

3 Move one foot to the side and stretch up wide again. Show me your beautiful, wide 'X' or star shape.

4 Slowly, continue bending low and stretching high and wide.

5 Lie on your back in a long, firm, stretched shape. Feel your toes reaching down and your hands reaching far above your head.

6 Bend both knees up, lift your head and back, and grasp hands round your knees. Slowly, continue lowering to a stretch shape and curling in to a rounded shape.

7 Try this stretching and curling while lying on one side and feel how your whole body is taking part.

8 Let's join all three stretchings and bendings, starting with the standing. (After the third bend, they sit and lie back, stretched. After the third stretch and bend on back, they roll over on to one side. After the third stretch and bend on side, they roll on to front and stand to repeat the three-part sequence.)

MOVEMENT SKILLS TRAINING - 15 minutes

1 Stand in lines of four, two boys and two girls, behind a leader. In 'The Snake' the leader's actions ripple down your snake's body as each person passes on the action. Keep one metre apart so that you can see the action of the person in front. Leader, show a clear action as you take your team away . . . . go!

2 Keep repeating your neat, clear action, leaders. Are your feet together, apart, or passing each other?

3 Stop! Well done, leaders and teams. Most of you kept together well and looked for good spaces. Leader, go to the end of the snake. New leader, please give us a new action and try to make your body shape firm and clear. With the music . . . . go!

4 Stop! Well done, leaders. I saw wide bouncing; tip toes, stretched walking; and firm, stretched arms in skipping. Change again. New leader, try an interesting new action (e.g. slither, slide, chasse, hopscotch, swing leg across, to one side or behind). Go!

5 Stop! Thank you for those excellent travelling ideas which I saw rippling down your snakes. Change over and let the last leader come to the front. Last leader, you might try an action, mostly on the move, but sometimes on the spot. All ready? Go!

DANCE - The Snake - 10 minutes

Music Any lively, jazzy, medium-to-fast tempo.

1 Snakes, I will call 'Change!' as the signal for the leaders to change. Leaders, travel carefully, always looking for good spaces. Snakes, keep together as your four actions ripple to your tail.

2 Stop! I will give each snake a number and ask each one, in turn, to demonstrate while all the other teams watch. Number one . . . . two . . . . three . . . . four . . . . everyone, go!

LESSON NOTES AND NC GUIDANCE

Pupils should be taught to:

a *respond to music.* To help them feel the music's beat, the teacher can chant rhythmically. The medium-speed, bouncy music usually breaks down easily into phrases of eight bars. 'Travel, travel, 3, 4, neat actions, 7, 8; keep together, space out well, 5, 6, 7, 8; 1, 2, 3, 4, 5, 6, leaders change.'

As well as keeping pupils with the music, such rhythmic accompaniment by the teacher can be used to improve the quality of the action. 'Softly, softly, into spaces, 5, 6, 7, 8; lively legs and swinging arms, 5, 6, 7, 8; bodies firm with nice strong shape, 5, 6, 7, 8.'

b *control movements by varying shape and size.* By making each of the four leaders responsible for a new aspect of movement, the class is made aware of some of the features of movement that make it interesting to perform and attractive to watch. Body shape variety with clear, firm use of body parts and small, neat, quiet movements contrasting, for example, with larger, livelier, more vigorous travelling movements, can be taught, experienced and understood in this lesson.

Lesson Plan – 30 minutes

Theme:
Fireworks.

WARM-UP ACTIVITIES - 5 minutes

1 We started our last lesson with big, slow, bending and stretching movements on the spot. Can you now balance, tall and stretched on tip toes, then run a few steps, jump up high, and show me another stretch in the air, keeping hands and feet together? Off you go!

2 Shoot your hands right up to the ceiling, like a rocket in space. Land softly with a nice 'give' in your knees and ankles.

3 Stand with feet and arms apart, high above your head – in the star shape that rockets make when they explode. Now, run a few steps and shoot straight up into another, beautifully wide star shape as you explode. Then land gently, squashing down carefully.

MOVEMENT SKILLS TRAINING - 15 minutes

1 Well done. I liked your straight and wide shapes in the air.

2 Before rockets 'Whoosh' into take-off, they have to be lit. Crouch low in a long, thin shape and pretend I have just lit your paper fuse. Show me your sizzling, starting actions.

3 Run into space for your take-off, 'Whoosh', and show me your explosion into a star shape, followed by your squashy landing.

4 From whooshing rockets, let's change to sparkling sparklers and hold one in each hand. Shake your hands quickly as you light up all the spaces around you, above, to sides, behind, high and low. Let your fingers shoot out and in quickly, like sparks flying.

5 Your hands can reach to different spaces at the same time or they can come together to make a double lot of sparks. Surprise me with your exciting, wandering spark makers.

6 From hands to feet now as you show me the actions of the little bangers that surprise us with their sudden, unexpected jumps. Jump quickly, sometimes on the spot, sometimes zig-zagging. I will be listening for your sudden quick movement sounds, 'Bang! Bang! Bang! . . . . Bang! . . . . Bang! . . . . Bang! Bang!' Go!

1 What brilliant 'Bangs!' For our 'Fireworks' dance, choose which firework you want to be. Hands up . . . . rockets . . . . sparklers . . . . bangers.

2 Sparklers go first, as you often do at firework parties, and keep going. Rockets, get ready.

3 Rockets, sizzle, whoosh and bang into star shapes, then drift slowly down. Keep repeating your performance. Bangers, get ready.

4 Lively, noisy bangers, off you go. Rockets and sparklers, keep going as well.

5 Rockets . . . . stop. Sparklers . . . . stop. Bangers . . . . stop.

6 Join hands in groups of four. You can hold hands with the two people next to you in a circle, or all put your right hand in to make a star. As Catherine wheels, circle round slowly, once, with all groups moving clockwise. Then, do one complete circle, speeding up a little. Then slow down gradually for one circle, drop hands and scatter, sinking to the floor.

7 Well done. In our next practice, show me how your rocket, sparkler or banger moves in its own special way. As Catherine wheels, do one slow, one speeding up and one slowing down circle, only.

LESSON NOTES AND NC GUIDANCE

Pupils should be taught to:

a *adopt the best possible posture and use of the body.* Through body movement in Dance we can express many things – moods, feelings and ideas. A firework display is the idea expressed here as we make the long, thin rocket's starting and flying shape, followed by its explosion into our biggest ever scattering body shape. The 'best possible posture and use of the body' is demonstrated through the starting shapes, actions and endings of each of the fireworks. Pupils are 'talking' to us through their body shapes and movements, often encouraged by the teacher's 'Show me your starting shape to tell me (express to me) which of the fireworks you are representing. Now show me the special ways of moving that we expect in your firework.' The focus is on the body's shape, size, tension, posture and use.

Pupils should be taught to:

a *compose and control their movements by varying shape, size, level, speed and tension.* Teacher commentary and praise for good work will specify what is good about a performance so that the class will develop and extend their work. 'I like your quick fingers and hands shaking and flying, high and low, to all the spaces around you, Ann. Well done.' 'Alan's Catherine wheel team joined up the slow start, the high-speed middle, and the gradual slow ending beautifully. Well done.'

Lesson Plan – 30 minutes

Theme:
Christmas.

WARM-UP ACTIVITIES - 5 minutes

1 At Christmas time there is lots of travelling and meeting friends. Travel to the bouncy music, and visit every part of the room – sides, ends, corners as well as the middle. Go!

2 Keep travelling. When I sound the tambourine twice, meet, join up and dance with someone near you. You may say 'Hello!'

3 Keep together, travelling neatly. When I strike the tambourine once, dance by yourself. You may say 'Goodbye!'

4 Two beats on the tambourine means meet and join up with a partner, but not the same one again. 'Hello!' (Keep repeating.)

MOVEMENT SKILLS TRAINING - 15 minutes

1 In our last lesson our muscles worked to keep the rockets firm and strong. Pretend you have no muscles. You are all dangling bones. Show me your floppy travelling.

2 You should be feeling all floppy. Can you feel your arms, neck and shoulders joining the rattling, started by the legs moving?

3 On the spot, move your bones slowly to go from one floppy shape to another. Feel as if you are using no energy in your loose shapes. Pretend you are a skeleton, rattling from shape to shape.

4 Puppets move like you, rattling and loose. Sit and sag like a puppet. When I name a body part, pretend I am pulling a string attached to that part and lift it jerkily like a puppet. Left knee! Right elbow! Both shoulders! Whole body pulled by neck and shoulders! Slowly crumple down to your saggy starting position.

5 What kind of Christmas present puppet would you want to be – soldier, doll, clown, fairy, robot or dancer? Decide. Then start off, lying on the floor. Pretend someone is lifting you slowly with strings, then holding you just high enough to let you do your jerky, loose, puppet movements. Soldiers, dolls, clowns, fairies, robots, dancers or whatever, please rise and dance.

6 Stop in a shape that tells me what kind of puppet you have been, and slowly, jerkily, sag down to your starting position.

1 The puppet maker is very sad. The puppets he (or she) has made for Christmas do not move properly. He cannot understand why.

2 The puppet maker walks up and down the lines of puppets on the shelves of the workshop. He stops often, lifts the imaginary strings of one or more puppets to bring them into action. The actions are poor, tired-looking and always too slow. The sad puppet maker moves on to a different group but they are just as poor. The sad puppet maker lies down, falls asleep and dreams.

3 Individuals, partners or small groups open their eyes, look keen and enthusiastic and rise up to sitting and standing position. With great style, they perform their distinctive, larger than life, floppy, loose dances, ending in a held shape before lowering back down to their sagging, limp positions on the floor.

4 The dancers become still. The puppet maker wakens, sits up and looks around him for the puppets with their excellent actions. All he sees are the same, poor, disappointing puppets.

LESSON NOTES AND NC GUIDANCE

Pupils should be taught to:

a *create simple characters and narratives.* The teacher's questioning focuses on the ways that pupils move to represent and express the puppets. 'Which body part is leading? Show me the slow lift and the opposite, quick flop. Show me, by your starting shape, which kind of puppet you want to be. What will be special about your soldier puppet's marching?'

b *express feelings, moods and ideas.* The puppet maker will express his or her slowness, sadness, disappointment and tiredness through body movements associated with such moods and feelings – the bowed back and dragging feet; the drooping arm gestures and shoulder shrugging; the sagging, drooping whole body down to the lying, sleeping.

The puppets will also express their characteristics through their movements – the swaggering soldier; the erratic clown; the neat and dainty fairy; the floppy doll; the stiff, almost jointless robot.

Lesson Plan – 30 minutes

Theme:
Winter.

WARM-UP ACTIVITIES - 5 minutes

1 January is often the coldest month. Let's pretend we are coming to school and moving to keep warm. Please join in the singing.

This is the way we rub and run (fast little steps and quick rubbing of chest, upper arms, shoulders), *rub and run, rub and run, this is the way we rub and run on a cold and frosty morning.*

This is the way we walk and shake (quick, lively, big shakes of legs and arms), *walk and shake, walk and shake, this is the way we walk and shake on a cold and frosty morning.*

(Repeat, then invite suggestions for other actions from the class. Hug and skip; shake and bounce; bend and stretch.)

MOVEMENT SKILLS TRAINING - 15 minutes

1 Each of my two cards has three winter words for you to think about, before deciding which set of words to choose.

Card 1 (Stream) RUSH   FREEZE   SKATE

Card 2 (Snow) FLOAT DRIFT   MELT

2 What kind of movement does the rushing stream make you think of? Bubbling and splashing; hurrying and spreading; sometimes crashing over stones. Show me your rushing.

3 Will the 'Freeze' be sudden or gradual? Gradual, becoming smoother, steadier, firmer, still, hard, jagged. Rush for three or four seconds, then start your freezing. Go!

4 Well done, frozen streams. Skating can be performed expertly with never a stumble, or inexpertly with lots of wobbly arm waving. Brilliant or wobbly . . . . off you go!

5 Snowflakes now. Can you tell me how they float down? Lightly; gently fluttering; then softly landing. Show me how you might slowly float, going from space to space, before coming to rest.

6 Those were excellent, gentle, snowflake movements. Well done. If your snowflake is suddenly struck by a strong wind, how will it respond and drift? High and low; with changes of direction; with pauses between gusts; with sudden, fast movements; all before settling, still in a snowflake shape. Ready for the wind? Drift!

7 When the snow melts into a puddle on the ground, it will be a slow and smooth movement, spreading outwards. Start in your snowflake shape, with parts of your body off the floor. Now melt slowly.

1 Hands up the 'stream words' group. Hands up the 'snowflakes' group.

2 Show me your starting shape which should tell me if you are going to rush or float – two very different actions.

3 I will call out the pairs of words to guide your timing. Rush or float . . . . freeze or drift . . . . skate or melt . . . .

4 Hold your final position, please, with the skaters in a clever or awkward position and shape.

LESSON NOTES AND NC GUIDANCE

Pupils should be:

• *involved in the continuous process of planning, performing and evaluating.* This is an excellent opportunity for planning because the performance of the three actions is short, and for performing because there is ample time for practising, repeating and remembering the little sequence. Pupils can then reflect on the performance by the other half of the class. Helpful suggestions are invited to bring about an improvement.

Such observations by pupils are valuable because the teacher is not always able to see everything going on. Performances are enhanced as pupils try hard to be selected for praise from observers.

Pupils should be taught to:

• *compose and control their movements by varying shape, size, direction, level, speed and tension.* Speed and tension contrasts are evident in the rushing of the stream and the gentle floating of the snowflake. The hard, jagged frozen water shapes contrast with the loose, spreading snowflakes. The high and low level and direction changes of the snowflakes in flight can be matched by the erratic skating of an inexpert novice.

Awareness of the elements of movement quality, variety and contrast are able to be taught and experienced in this lesson.

Lesson Plan – 30 minutes

Theme:
Traditional, folk dance style, creative dance.

WARM-UP ACTIVITIES - 5 minutes

1 Dance on the spot for eight counts, then travel through good spaces for the next eight counts.

2 'On the spot' can include skipping, setting or bouncing in time with the music. Let your travelling really go somewhere as a good contrast. On the spot, 3, 4, 5, 6, 7, now travel; 1, 2, travelling well, 5, 6, now on the spot.

3 Find a partner. One of you show your dancing on the spot to the other and both remember it. Then the other partner shows their travelling for both to practise and remember.

4 Decide whether to dance side by side, or following the leader as you perform your shared choice.

TEACH ONE COUPLE FIGURES TO BE LINKED CREATIVELY - 15 minutes

Partner on the left as couple face top of set is A. Partner on the right is B. Each figure takes eight bars of the music.

1 Dance round partner and back. A dances round the front of B and back to place, four counts. B repeats round A, dancing for four counts.

2 Cast off on own side (A turns to left, B turns to right) and dance to bottom for four counts. Turn in, join hands to dance to top and back to own places.

3 Change places with partner, four counts, giving right hands, then four to change back to own places, giving left hands.

4 Dance down middle of set, four counts, with hands joined, turn and dance back to top and own places, four counts.

5 Back to back or Do-si-do. Both go forwards, passing right shoulders, and back, passing left shoulders, without turning body round, i.e. keep facing partner's side of dance. Four counts each way.

COUPLES PLAN AND PRACTISE OWN 32-BAR DANCE - 10 minutes

Music Any 32-bar, English or Scottish country dance.

Formation Sets of one couple.

Each person can select two of the five figures opposite that he or she wishes to include in their four-figure dance. Both partners share in deciding the order of the figures to ensure a neat, smooth flow from figure to figure; variety in direction and in being joined or separate; and an ending that appeals to both.

LESSON NOTES AND NC GUIDANCE

Pupils should be taught to:

a *respond to music.* With beginners we use slightly quicker music, and they can be asked to 'Stand still and clap your hands in time with this folk dance music' before going into their warm-up activities. The music is phrased in groups of eight bars and the teacher's rhythmic accompaniment and chanting of the actions helps the class to 'feel' the music and to keep with it. 'On the spot, lively movements, 5, 6, now you travel; travel, travel, lively travel, 5, 6, on the spot.'

Taking exactly eight bars for each figure of the dance is most important, so that pupils arrive back and go straight into the next figure without needing to mark time if early, or dash in, in poor style, if late. Once again, the teacher can keep them with the music by accompanying each figure. 'Cast off, own side, 3, meet and turn, up the middle, hands joined, back to starting places.'

b *perform a number of dances from different times and places, including some traditional dances of the British Isles.* In this easy introduction to folk dance the pupils are learning actual steps and figures from English and Scottish dances, and their own created dances are folk dances in style and pattern.

Lesson Plan – 30 minutes

Theme:
Traditional folk dance.

WARM-UP ACTIVITIES - 5 minutes

1 Skip by yourself, visiting every part of the room.

2 If the floor is suddenly crowded, keep skipping on the spot, then travel on when there is plenty of room.

3 Skip for eight counts, then join hands with someone and dance for eight counts. After these eight counts, separate and dance by yourself for eight counts. Then take a different partner for the next eight counts.

4 By yourself, 3, 4, 5, 6, join a partner. Hands joined, 3, 4, 5, 6, 7, split up. By yourself, 3, 4, 5, 6, find a new partner. Dance together, 3, 4, 5, 6, now split up. On your own, 3, 4, 5, 6, 7, 8.

TEACH FIGURES OF NEW DANCE - Cumberland Reel - 15 minutes

Formation Longways set of two couples.

1 Couples right and left hand star. Right hand to dancer diagonally opposite and wheel round for four counts. Left hand to dancer diagonally opposite and dance back to starting places. On the left hand wheel, break the star on count three to let you finish in your own places on count four.

2 First couple dance down the centre and back to their place. Assist each other with your right hands. Going down, turn on count four to give you time to return to top of set on count three, to be in your own places on count four.

3 Both couples face top of set for casting to left and right. A casts to the left, B casts to the right. Second couple follow. First couple make an arch at the bottom, the second couple go under and promenade to top of set, hands joined. First couple follow.

4 All promenade round to the left with the second couple leading, back to set formation where the new first couple can start.

DANCE - Cumberland Reel - 10 minutes

Music   *Cumberland Reel* by Blue Mountain Band (EFDS), from *Community Dances Manual 1*, or any 32-bar dance.

Formation   Longways set of four, five or six couples.

Bars 1–8
Two top couples right and left hand star.

Bars 9–16
First couple dance down the centre and back.

Bars 17–24
A casts left and B casts right, others following. First couple make an arch at the bottom, others go under the arch and promenade up the centre to top of set.

Bars 25–32
All promenade round to the left, followed by first couple.

Repeat with new first and second couples doing the right and left hand star.

LESSON NOTES AND NC GUIDANCE

Pupils should be taught to:

b *perform a number of dances from different times and places, including some traditional dances of the British Isles.* Because the figures of the dance involve two couples only, it is taught in two couple sets to involve the whole class. Within this formation, each of the couples has a turn at being first couple, that is the couple nearer the top of the set, and a turn at being second couple.

In the long set of four or more couples, each first couple leads the dance once only, and then finishes in bottom place while a new first couple re-starts the dance. This is an easy dance with both Scottish and English versions.

Pupils should demonstrate that they can:

a *work safely as members of a team.* Working sensibly, safely and co-operatively; being in the right place at the right time; not pushing and shoving others; and trying to dance neatly in time with the music, are all essential elements of an enjoyable and successful folk dance lesson.

b *repeat sequences with increasing control and accuracy.* The ability to remember and repeat a series or sequence of linked actions or movements is a prime National Curriculum requirement. This dance, with its four-part repeating pattern, gives excellent practice in the thinking ahead required for a successful performance. The teacher will ensure that there is a special focus during each practice to ensure improvement.

Lesson Plan – 30 minutes

Theme:
Body contact sounds and rhythms.

WARM-UP ACTIVITIES - 5 minutes

1 In our last lesson we danced in time with folk dance music. Let's travel to some folk dance music and feel the sets of eight counts. By yourselves . . . . go!

2 Can you include some kind of change for each set of eight counts? Travel; dance on the spot; change the action; or change direction.

3 This time, ignore one set of eight beats and stand still. Then join in again, exactly in time with the music, eight bars later. At any one time, some of you will be standing, quietly counting up to eight, while all the others are travelling around. Go!

MOVEMENT SKILLS TRAINING - 15 minutes

1 Sit down and listen to the nursery rhyme I am sounding with my hands and feet. Please do not shout out if you know which one it is. Listen, and then put your hand up to tell me.

2 *Jack and Jill went up the hill* is sounded with hands on the floor. *To fetch a pail of water* is sounded with feet beating on the floor. *Jack fell down and broke his crown* is sounded with cupped hands on opposite shoulders, arms crossed. *And Jill came tumbling after* uses hands and feet on the floor.

3 After identifying the nursery rhyme, the pupils remain seated, say the words and accompany the teacher in sounding them out on floor, hands and shoulders.

4 Stand and sing out the first line, making a rhythmic clapping of hands. You can walk forwards, rising up on tip toes. *Jack and Jill went up the hill.*

5 Sound feet strongly on the spot. *To fetch a pail of water.*

6 On *Jack fell down and broke his crown,* clap hands, starting high and coming down (like Jack) with a huge clap on crown.

7 *And Jill came tumbling after,* skipping with crossed-arm handclaps from shoulders down to a final slap on thighs.

8 Well done. Let's practise again with every word accompanied by a hand or foot movement, sounding clearly. Sing, clap, dance . . . . go!

DANCE - Jack and Jill - 10 minutes

1 Find a partner and decide who is one and who is two.

2 On line one of the rhyme, one stays on the spot, making feet and hand sounds. Number two circles round one, with lively feet beating the floor and hands slapping sides or thighs. *Jack and Jill went up the hill.*

3 On line two, change over and repeat, as for line one. *To fetch a pail of water.*

4 On line three, partners face each other, with hands high, do small galloping steps to same side, and clap, bringing hands low for a loud clap on crown. Jack fell down and broke his crown.

5 *And Jill came tumbling after.* Partners, still face each other, clap own hands twice, (and Jill); clap own knees, (came tumbling); then clap each other's hands at head height (after).

6 **Development.** Partners can create their own short, body rhythms dance to a different nursery rhyme. Pairs demonstrate and others try to identify the new nursery rhyme.

LESSON NOTES AND NC GUIDANCE

Pupils should be taught to:

a *try hard to consolidate their performances and gain a sense of achievement.* Performances will only be improved and consolidated if the teacher works hard at demanding neat, controlled actions, provides ample opportunities for practice, looks out for and comments on good quality work, and uses demonstrations to identify the main features being pursued.

Pupils should be taught to:

b *respond to a range of stimuli, through Dance.* In the same way that a Dance lesson should include variety and contrast for maximum interest, a Dance programme should include many kinds of inspirations to make the series of lessons interesting, relevant, seasonal, challenging, surprising and exciting. In addition to music which is widely used, sound as a stimulus can be provided by percussion instruments; the chanting of the rhythm of words, phrases, names, place names, numbers, food; action songs and rhymes; and by using body contact sounds with nursery rhymes, as here.

Varied stimuli also include: actions; flash cards; objects; moods and feelings; nature; stories; seasonal events and festivals; work actions; pictures; outings; animals; numbers; work going on in class; and things of particular interest to teacher and class.

Lesson Plan – 30 minutes

Theme Circus.

Music TV Sport from Festival of Music by Central Band of the R.A.F.

WARM-UP ACTIVITIES - 6 minutes

1 For our parade into town, march anti-clockwise in a big circle. Wave to the towns-people. 'Hello! We're back. Come and see us.'

2 Join hands in a big circle. From a low starting position, travel forwards to a medium height, tent shape, then back to your circle. On your second go, travel forwards and make a high tent shape on tip toes.

3 **Trapezists** Space out in one half of the room, facing the other half of the class. With high, stretched arms, travel forwards, swinging to a high level. Swing back to a lower level. Repeat.

4 **Tightrope walkers** Each half of the class faces a different side of the room. Hold your arms sideways for your wobbly balance. Balance step forwards, forwards, wobble, wobble; balance step back, back, wobble, wobble. Repeat.

MOVEMENT SKILLS TRAINING - 12 minutes

1 In our groups of four, decide which circus actions you will make into a pattern you can remember and repeat. Will you be clowns, jugglers, trapezists, acrobats, tightrope walkers, strong men or women, or will you be the band?

2 Let your actions show the main feature of the circus people. For example, the strong man or woman pulling the imaginary rope dragging the others along, expresses 'Pull them hard, pull them strong, look at my muscles, look at my muscles (flexing biceps).'

3 Clowns might do a funny walk on heels, spin round with one leg high, fall down slowly, bounce up quickly, and keep repeating it.

4 Tightrope walkers and trapezists can use the sequence we did earlier in the lesson or bring in your own ideas.

5 Jugglers, you can juggle in front, in front; overhead, overhead; up the back, up the back.

6 Whatever you decide, remember to make a short, three- or four-part pattern that you can repeat. While you are practising it, one of you may say the actions to remind your group.

1 Parade, anti-clockwise, round in a big circle.

2 Hands should be joined in the circle to make the big top.

3 Members of class at opposite ends of the room face each other as they trapeze forwards and backwards, twice.

4 Members of class facing opposite sides of the room perform the wobbly tightrope walker's balance walk forwards and backwards.

5 In groups of four, perform own circus actions.

6 Lowering of big top. All hands joined in a circle, high on tip toes, in a high tent shape. All travel back, hands still joined, lowering down and back. Then all travel forwards to a medium height, half lowered tent shape, then travel all the way back, lowering tent right down to floor.

7 Parade out of town. Transfer from lowered tent, circle shape, to the big circle, leaving town, clockwise, waving 'Goodbye. We'll see you next year.'

LESSON NOTES AND NC GUIDANCE

Pupils should be taught to:

a *create simple characters and narratives.* The expression of the identity of the characters being created is done through our bodily movements. We are not miming, acting or contorting our facial muscles. Our whole body is being used to represent the style of movement we associate with the characters. Their typical actions, shapes, amount of effort used and any particular idiosyncrasies are all included in the movement expression.

Pupils should be able to show that they can:

a *respond imaginatively to the various challenges.* The start and finish of this dance are teacher-directed. The middle of the dance involves the groups of four in deciding which of the work actions they want to perform, and then planning to incorporate those actions into an easily remembered repeating pattern.

b *repeat sequences with increasing control and accuracy.* Each group of four is helped and encouraged to plan its repeating pattern of actions to provide interest, variety and contrast. The sequence is short enough to be easily remembered and repeated and long enough to give a good expression of the characters, as in the teacher-led, tightrope walkers' sequence in the warm-up.

Lesson Plan – 30 minutes

Theme:
Traditional folk dance.

WARM-UP ACTIVITIES - 5 minutes

1 Partners, decide who is one and who is two. Travel, side by side, with number one deciding what to do and where to do it. Change the action after each set of eight bars of music. A change of direction, also on eight, always looks attractive.

2 Number two, can you decide on actions to take you apart, and then bring you together again, allowing eight counts for each?

3 Partners, practise a four-part, repeating A : B : B : A pattern of travelling together; parting, closing; parting, closing; and travelling together.

TEACH AND DANCE - Djatchko Kolo (Yugoslavian Folk Dance) - 20 minutes

Music *Djatchko Kolo*, Society for International Folk Dancing (cassette and book 3).
Formation Open circle with teacher at the right hand open end.
This simple dance can be learned easily with the teacher calling out and demonstrating each movement straight away with the music, with the class copying the teacher.

Figure 1	**Bar 1**	**Beat 1**	Step right foot to right.
		2	Close left foot to right foot.
		3	Step right foot to right.
		4	Swing left foot across right foot.
	Bar 2	**Beats 1–4**	Repeat **bar 1** to the left, starting with left foot.
	Bars 3 & 4		Repeat all of above.
Figure 2	**Bar 5**	**Beat 1**	Step right foot to right.
		2	Swing left foot across right foot.
		3	Step left foot to left.
		4	Swing right foot across left foot.
	Bar 6	**Beats 1–4**	Repeat **bar 5**.
Figure 3	**Bars 7 & 8**		Starting with right foot, perform seven little walking steps to the right and point heel of right foot on floor on the last beat of **bar 8**.
	Bars 9 & 10		Seven steps to left and point heel of left foot on the floor, on the last beat of **bar 10**.

Keep repeating the dance from the beginning.

REVISE A FAVOURITE DANCE - 5 minutes

This can be a folk dance such as the 'Cumberland Reel' or, for variety, a creative dance such as 'Circus' of the previous month.

LESSON NOTES AND NC GUIDANCE

Pupils should be taught to:

a *be physically active.* The challenge for the teacher is to 'get on with it' by keeping explanations clear and short; by being confident that the class can keep up with him or her in going through this easy dance; and by rhythmically accompanying the actions, while dancing with the pupils in the circle. 'Step to right, close, step right, swing left; step to left, close, step left, swing right.' Hearing the instructions and following the teacher's lead make this an easy dance to learn, with few stoppages.

b *perform a number of dances from different times and places.* With younger, less experienced dancers, teaching in a circle formation where all can see and be seen by the teacher is the easiest way. A dance from the 'different times and places' repertoire, will ideally be something to which interested members of staff might contribute. Many teachers will have no experience of folk dance from their schooldays or college training.

Pupils should be able to show that they can:

a *remember and repeat a series of movements performed previously.* Because this is such a simple dance, there should be ample time to include a favourite dance with which to finish the lesson. The class can be asked 'What dance shall we finish with?' to let the teacher see which are their particular favourites, or the teacher can decide to include a dance because it provides a good contrast with the one just learned.

Lesson Plan – 30 minutes

Theme:
Fast and slow.

WARM-UP ACTIVITIES - 5 minutes

1 Can you be very clever and show me a leg action on the spot; then a short travel; then big body movements, such as bending, stretching, twisting, rising or lowering, on the spot?

2 Show me your starting position for your first action, with arms, legs and body nicely balanced and ready. Begin!

3 Stop! Now look for a good space for your short travelling action. I hope it's different to the first action. Ready? Go!

4 Stop! On the spot, show me your one or two whole body movements.

5 Stop in a held shape. Well done. Keep practising all three actions again in your own time. Show me your still shape at the start and finish, each time. Off you go!

MOVEMENT SKILLS TRAINING - 10 minutes

1 Stand ready, again, for your first leg action on the spot. Pretend the floor is hot and do the action as fast as you can. Go!

2 Stop! Now, do your travelling action at equally high speed to take you to a space. Make every part of your body join in.

3 On the spot, find a good balance position for your high speed body movements – up and down, in and out, round and back, go!

4 Wow! You looked like out-of-control machines. Well done. Now, like machines with almost no power, do your three actions in ultra-slow motion, just moving and no more. Slowmo . . . . go!

5 Use your joints fully to make your slow motion a whole body slow motion. Don't cut down on the size of your actions. Once again, v-e-e-r-y slo-o-ow-ly, begin!

DANCE - Fast Forwards, Fast Back, Slow Motion Replay - 15 minutes

1 Find a partner. I want you both to think about a favourite TV sport that you might like to perform in an unusual dance.

2 Performers, show me by your starting shape what your sport is. I see swimmers, cricketers, golfers, footballers, tennis and netball players, athletes, jockeys, skiers, canoeists, gliders, hockey and rugby players, and weight lifters. What brilliant variety.

3 Off you go. Practise your chosen sport and see if you can make a little repeating pattern of three or four parts that's easy to remember (e.g. forehand, backhand, run in and smash; or jump, catch, run in and score; or swing, swing, hit the golf ball).

4 One of you stand ready to perform. Partner, sit down. Pretend you are about to watch sport on TV. As you press the control buttons, say 'normal' or 'fast forwards' or 'fast back' or 'slow motion', and your sporty partner must immediately respond. Be sensible, please, and don't use 'fast back' or 'fast forwards' for more than a few seconds. Over to you, operators. Begin.

5 Stop! Sportspersons, sit down beside your operators and tell them what you thought of their button pushing. How would you like them to change to help you perform better?

6 Same dancers and operators. One more improved practice, please.

7 Well done, dancers and operators. That looked much better. Now, change duties and we'll do the whole thing again twice.

8 Half of the class can now enjoy watching the other half.

LESSON NOTES AND NC GUIDANCE

Pupils should be able to:

a *respond to a range of stimuli, through Dance.* The remote control for their television, and the many sporting events on TV are well known, relevant stimuli for most modern youngsters. Paradoxically, these stimuli in real life are combining to destroy regular pupil participation in sporting activity.

b *respond imaginatively to the various challenges.* The pupils are given full responsibility for deciding their sport and planning the actions to be represented. Responses will be original, and, with teacher encouragement, might become imaginative.

Pupils should be able to show that they can:

a *make simple judgements about their own and others' performances.* It is important to provide opportunities for observing demonstrations when pupils have worked so hard at planning and practising something original. Encouraging, friendly, helpful comments give pleasure to the performers and inspire them to further improvement. Comments made often have relevance for others.

Lesson Plan – 30 minutes

Theme:
Feelings.

WARM-UP ACTIVITIES - 5 minutes

1 I am sure that you will include 'Happy' among your end of school year feelings as we come to the summer holidays. Please join me in singing the words as we do our lively skipping, marching or bouncing around.

If you're happy and you know it, clap your hands,
If you're happy and you know it, clap your hands,
If you're happy and you know it, and you really want to show it,
If you're happy and you know it, clap your hands.

If you're happy and you know it . . . . swagger round, wave to friends, punch the air, bounce and bounce etc.

MOVEMENT SKILLS TRAINING - 15 minutes

1 Find a partner and sit down, together, with one piece of percussion to be used later. I want you to agree on three action words that might describe your first year in junior school. Word one might be a shy, quiet, unsure start, creeping or gliding on to your little stage. Word two will be more lively, self-confident, growing, stretching, spreading or gesturing. Word three, for the end of the year, might be any of the happy actions we have practised, or it might be quite a sad closing in on yourself or waving 'Goodbye' as you fade away.

2 Choose your three action words. Number one practise first with your partner watching carefully, ready to make a helpful suggestion for improvement. Let each action have a still start and finish position with a good body shape showing it off.

3 Sit down, number one, and listen to your partner's friendly advice. It might be about the action, shape, speed or timing. Having been helped, number one, perform again please.

4 Now change places to let number two practise the same three action words. Let your body movements tell us about your feelings and use your whole body as you do it.

5 Number two, sit down beside your partner to be given some friendly, helpful advice to improve your performance.

6 Number two, perform again and try to use the advice given.

DANCE - Feelings - 10 minutes

1 Number one, stand ready to perform your three actions. Number two, use the percussion quietly to accompany your partner. Start and stop the sound to make each action have a still start and finish position. Percussionist, take charge. Begin.

2 Well done. One more practice with the same dancer. Try your best.

3 Change places, please, and start when you are both ready. Practise twice and remember to separate the three actions.

4 Pairs will watch pairs now. Observers, try to guess what the three actions are. Each partner has a turn at performing.

5 You have all seen a couple performing and suggested what the three actions were. Let's look at several couples chosen for their interesting, excellent, clear and expressive performances.

LESSON NOTES AND NC GUIDANCE

Pupils should be taught to:

a *express feelings, moods and ideas.* The lesson might have been introduced by the teacher explaining 'In this month's lesson we are trying to express feelings and emotions by the way we move. We must only do this by the way we move.'

The physical expressions of happiness in the warm-up with the hand clapping, swaggering and waving etc., all focus on the whole body and the way it is moving.

Pupils should be able to show that they can:

a *respond imaginatively to the various challenges.* The challenges are 'shared choice'. The teacher suggests the nature of the three actions but the pupils decide on the exact responses and words and have ample opportunity to plan and perform imaginatively.

b *repeat sequences with increasing control and accuracy.* When the performance is as short as here, it is easy to repeat, adapt, practise, improve and remember one's sequence.

c *make simple judgements effectively to improve the accuracy, quality and variety of their own performance.* Partner work provides the best opportunity for someone to look at what you are doing, to comment on it, and to help you improve.

Lesson Plan – 30 minutes

Theme:
Basic actions.

WARM-UP ACTIVITIES - 5 minutes

1 Show me how quickly you respond to instructions and how good you are at finding spaces. Best walking . . . . go!

2 Stop! This time, travel along straight lines, never in a circle (this is common, usually anti-clockwise, in primary schools). When I stop you, take one step, if necessary, to find a space by yourself.

3 Stop! Move to a better space. Well done, everyone.

4 Now show me your best, quietest, neatest running, still along straight lines, never following anyone. Go!

5 In your own big space, stop! Now, let's look at some examples of really good, quiet running, always looking for good spaces.

MOVEMENT SKILLS TRAINING - 15 minutes

1 Follow me through the eleven actions on my chart. I will use six beats of the music to each action. Keep with me.

Heels bouncing
Whole body bouncing
Walking forwards
Walking backwards
Skipping
Running
Running on the spot
Stamping feet
Clapping hands
Clapping body parts
Clapping hands with partner

2 In our next practice of all the actions, work hard to make your shape strong and firm, with no 'saggy', lazy arms, legs or body.

3 Well done. Now sit down with a partner and plan a four-part sequence which must end with 'clapping hands with partner.'

4 Include a variety of actions, some on the spot, some travelling. A direction change provides an interesting contrast. When you have agreed, stand up and practise to the music.

Music Medium-to-quick, bouncy, rhythmic.

1 Let's all work together to my counting. Ready? Go! First action, 3, 4, 5 and change; second action, 3, 4, 5 and change; third action, 3, 4, 5 and change; clapping partner's hands, 4, 5, start again.

2 Stop! Well done. Decide now where you will go. Will you be one behind the other, side by side, or a mixture? Do you change direction somewhere? Do you part and close? Does one dance on the spot while the other travels? Ready to try again? Go!

3 Well done. I saw some excellent partnerships. Let's have half of the class looking at the other half. Look out for and tell me which pairs you like and why. Look for neat, quiet movements and pairs working and keeping together well – and maybe surprising you with their clever use of space.

LESSON NOTES AND NC GUIDANCE

Pupils should be taught to:

a *recognise the safety risks of inappropriate clothing, jewellery and footwear.* Long trousers catch heels; watches and rings can impact against others and cause serious scarring and injury; large fashionable trainers are noisy, ungiving, often filthy, and should be banned indoors. Barefoot work is recommended because it is quiet, looks neat, and uses the small, under-used muscles of feet and ankles as they support, balance, propel and receive the body weight. Long hair should be bunched back to stop it impeding vision.

b *respond readily to instructions.* Now is the time, with a new class, to put a stop to bad behaviour, particularly in classes that do not respond immediately to requests to start or stop; who rush around selfishly and noisily, disturbing others; who are never quiet in their work; and who do not try to move well, destroying any prospects for high standards or lesson enjoyment by the majority of pupils and the teacher.

Pupils should be able to show that they can:

a *practise, improve and refine performance.* As well as the message 'This is the way we dress and behave in our Physical Education lessons,' the teacher should set the highest standards for the way that pupils participate. We want wholehearted, vigorous and almost non-stop activity, inspired and guided by a well-prepared, enthusiastic teacher. Teaching will identify the features of good quality work; praise will encourage the praised to greater effort; and demonstrations of good work will set a standard to aim for.

Deep breathing and perspiration, seldom experienced in the inactive lifestyles of many of today's youngsters, should be evident.

Lesson Plan – 30 minutes

Theme:
Awareness of space.

WARM-UP ACTIVITIES - 5 minutes

1 As you travel from space to space with my shaking tambourine, use some of the actions we met in the last lesson, or different ones such as gallop, slide, rush, creep, float, leap or hurry. Perform short travels and stop on the loud beat of the tambourine . . . . go!

2 Use your eyes while you are still to look for your next good space. Variety in travelling actions, please. Go!

3 On each of the many stops, show me a well-balanced, whole body shape where parts of you reach out into the spaces in front, above, to the sides and behind you, high and low.

4 Well done, travellers and reachers into space.

MOVEMENT SKILLS TRAINING - 15 minutes

1 Stand in your own place, well away from anyone. Note where you are. There might be a mark on the floor, or you might be in line with a window or a door. Show me how your clever feet can travel away from your spot and return to the exact same place, exactly sixteen counts later. Go! 1, 2, 3, 4 (up to) 13, 14, 15, 16 and still!

2 Let's try again. Show me your varied actions and all the parts of the hall that you can visit in sixteen counts exactly. Go!

3 As well as visiting many parts of the room, can you reach out and touch the space around you, at different levels (high leaps, low slithering, medium arm swing turns).

4 Now show me how many movements you can do in sixteen counts without moving away from your spot on the floor. Arms, legs, head, shoulders, and back can all bend, stretch, twist, reach, swing into all the spaces surrounding you.

5 Some movements, like a long stretching, can be slow, taking several counts. Others can swing or reach out quickly into space. Play around with the speed of your big body movements.

DANCE - Space Travel - 10 minutes

1 Find a partner and stand next to each other. Decide who will be number one and who will be number two.

2 While I sound out the sixteen counts, number one will move on the spot and number two will travel through space. Both will finish, still, in an attractive shape. Ready? Begin.

3 1, 2, 3 . . . . 13, 14, 15, 16, be still. Show me your firm shape.

4 Now number two will move on the spot and number one will travel. Be together again on count sixteen. Go! 1, 2, 3 . . . . 15 . . . . and still.

5 Let's spend a little time looking at our partner's actions on the spot, and then travelling. One can perform while the other watches and then we'll change over. This will help you to plan actions that are different to your partner's for variety.

6 Now, we'll do the whole thing twice through, working together.

7 Half of the class will watch the other half demonstrating. Look for and tell me about neat, varied movements and any really good examples of travelling for sixteen counts exactly.

LESSON NOTES AND NC GUIDANCE

Pupils should be taught to:

a *be mindful of others.* Space awareness is the same as awareness of other people. In a small room filled with fast moving pupils, it is essential to train the class to move safely, sensibly and co-operatively. The teacher often has to train the class not to travel round anti-clockwise, in a big circle, with everyone following and being impeded by others, typical in many primary schools. Accidents seldom happen with a class trained to travel on straight lines; visiting all parts of the room; never following the pathway of another; looking before changing directions; and sometimes running on the spot until a space appears.

Pupils should show that they can:

a *repeat sequences with increasing control and accuracy.* The requirement to practise, improve, remember and be able to repeat a series of linked movements is a main feature of the National Curriculum. Implicit in this is the need to be involved in the continuous process of thinking ahead to plan an intended outcome; then performing wholeheartedly in a focused, poised way; then reflecting on the success of the work as a guide to repeating the whole process.

Lesson Plan – 30 minutes

Theme:
Autumn.

WARM-UP ACTIVITIES - 5 minutes

1 In our last lesson your travelling was vigorous with strong steps, runs or jumps. Our movements on the spot were mostly firm stretching, bending, twisting or punching. Show me that you can also travel with light, gentle, floating movements – just like falling leaves in autumn. Lift up on to tip toes and float, hardly moving, with arms and upper body tilting, turning, slowly and gently. Keep going.

2 Pretend a gust of wind has just pushed you, making you glide more quickly along. Can your arms help you to glide and then tilt to curve round in a big, smooth turn?

3 The wind drops and the leaf drops, slowly floating down.

MOVEMENT SKILLS TRAINING - 10 minutes

1 Keep this feeling of lightness and let me see you swaying on the spot, almost floating in your own space. You may move one foot to give you a bigger reach out into space if you want. How far can you go forwards, back, or to the sides, just like a leaf still attached to its swaying branch?

2 Some movements will be jerky after a sudden gust of wind. Can you show me?

3 What is your leaf shape – wide, narrow, flat, curved, crinkly, twisted or jagged? Show me your flying movements and your shape which might change in the wind, still attached to your branch.

1 Our three-part dance will include: movements while attached to a branch; being blown from the branch and flying into space; and falling to the ground.

2 Let's all practise, one part at a time, using voice sounds as an accompaniment. On the branch, ready. Begin and wheeee . . . . wheeee . . . . gentle fluttering and turning and circling . . . . wheeee.

3 Good, and I liked your sensible, gentle 'wheeeeing'. Now the wind becomes stronger and stronger and blows the leaf, whoosh, out into space. Ready to fly . . . . go . . . . whoosh . . . . whoosh . . . . snap off . . . . gliding, soaring, turning, hovering.

4 Very well done, again, with some excellent sharing of the air space in our hall. Now the wind has stopped and the leaves will slowly, softly, gently float to the ground. Can you slowly, softly, safely lower, bit by bit, to the floor?

5 Practise lowering to the floor again. Do not use your hands to support your fall. Flow, bending sideways along the sides of legs, hips and upper body, keeping your head and hands out of the way.

6 Half of the class work in the centre (the wood?), and half sit round the outside as wind machines. Watching half, please help by providing a gentle wind, then a stormy gusty wind, and then silence. Dancers, show me your favourite leaf shape as you wait to start. Wind blowers, please start.

7 For our changeover, the wind blowers can walk carefully through the fallen leaves, pretending to kick them, rolling them to the sides where they will sit up and become the new wind blowers.

LESSON NOTES AND NC GUIDANCE

General Requirements. Pupils should be taught to:

a *adopt the best possible posture and use of the body.* When we perform travelling actions the first thought is 'What is or are the leg actions I am using? How are my feet and legs working to do the action neatly and correctly?' When we perform whole body movements, bending, stretching, twisting, curling or arching, our main thought is 'How am I holding and controlling my whole body posture and shape, particularly in the spine, head, arms and shoulders to represent and express the several movements?'

Programme of Study. Pupils should be able to:

a *compose and control their movements by varying shape, size, level, direction, speed and tension.* Expressing leaf-like movement requires the dancer to plan a starting shape and size on the tree, changing to new shapes and sizes in swift flight or gentle hovering. Changing levels, directions, speeds and feelings of vigorous flight or calm floating will all be encouraged, experienced and practised.

Lesson Plan – 30 minutes

Theme:
Voice sounds.

WARM-UP ACTIVITIES - 5 minutes

1 Find a partner for a 'quick thinking' warm-up. Travel together to this bouncy music with one of you being leader this week.

2 The leader's first responsibility is to find good spaces and plan the varied actions to be copied by the partner.

3 When I bang the drum, make a change. It might be a different action, change of direction, or it might be a new position – side by side, following, one on the spot, one circling round, or holding one, two or no hands. (Several drum beats should be sounded about ten seconds apart to give time for the changes to take place.)

4 Well done, quick thinking leaders. Watch these three couples whose quick responses and varied changes impressed me.

MOVEMENT SKILLS TRAINING - 15 minutes

1 Your 'wheeeeing' and 'whoooshing' wind sounds in the last lesson also impressed me. Say together the words on my card.

SIZZLE What pictures in your head does this word suggest? Show me how someone or something might move, if sizzling.

ZOOM What sort of action does this suggest? Slow or quick? If there is travelling, what will it be like? Show me.

BANG What words could describe this action? Will it be slow or gentle, or not? Show me your ideas.

BOING What pictures, if any, does this word produce for you? What sort of action is 'Boinging' like? Try to show me.

2 Keep practising by yourselves, moving to these words and saying them as you move. Try to express their speed and their force.

3 Re-arrange the order if you wish. Decide on a starting position which will be a good lead in to your first word. If you are moving like a rocket, motorbike, car, bullet, firework or whatever, try to show it in your starting position.

4 Let's have half the class looking at half the demonstrations to share good ideas. Look for good movement, actions that surprise you, and see if you can recognise what is being represented by the dancers.

5 After both sets of demonstrations and helpful, positive comments, there should be more class practice to let them use some of the good ideas and features seen and admired.

1 Find a partner and share your ideas to see if you can come up with a really good sequence, working together. Remember that it is not long; two of the actions, at least, are very short.

2 Are you going to say the words together, or will only one speak at a time? Together would be good, but how will you do it at exactly the same time?

3 Show good, clear actions and shapes and a change of direction, level, speed or force to make it even more interesting.

LESSON NOTES AND NC GUIDANCE

Pupils should be able to:

a *respond to a range of stimuli through Dance.* As stimuli, the four words concerned provide a double bonus. They can each inspire specific images – rocket, bullet, explosion, firework, sausages frying – and the image can inspire the idea for the movement. They can also be given a strong vocal accompaniment which is most enjoyable and gives the sequence a rhythm.

b *compose and control their movements by varying shape, size, level, direction, speed and tension.* Pupils will first be asked 'Can you show me your clear, firm starting shape for your four-part sequence, the body shapes within the actions concerned, and then try to hold and show me your finishing shape.' They will then be told 'A change of level or direction at some point will give interesting variety. Low sizzling rocket to high flight; high, crashed motor-cyclist to lying down flat.' Finally, they can be asked to think about the 'How?' of their movement. 'Will your actions be slow or quick, gentle or explosive, light or heavy? Can you surprise me with a sudden contrast?'

Pupils should be able to show that they can:

a *work safely in pairs. The partner work is totally partner-centred.* They have full responsibility for deciding and planning their sequence, the order of the actions, and how 'together' they will be in performing and adding vocal sounds. They need to work safely, carefully and considerately, not crashing into or disturbing other pairs. They need to be willing to listen to and consider the views of their partner.

Lesson Plan – 30 minutes

Theme:
Pathways and shapes.

WARM-UP ACTIVITIES - 5 minutes

1 Think of a shape or a letter in your name that you would like to draw on the floor in a tiny space, then repeat exactly using the whole floor space. When you have decided, let me see you walking your shape or letter, tiny, then room-size.

2 Return to your starting place after your long travel. Practise again, tiny and then as large as you can manage.

3 Can you use interesting travelling actions and neat turning, leaning or twisting into curving pathways? I am watching your feet taking you and your upper body guiding you.

MOVEMENT SKILLS TRAINING - 12 minutes

1 Don't rush into your answer! Think carefully. Can anyone be brilliant and tell me a number between 5 and 7?

2 Well done, Sarah, 6 is correct. Now, everyone, find a big space where you can travel and draw a capital 'S'. Show me your starting body shape and position. Will you lead with an arm, hand, shoulder or your back? You might even be starting, standing in an 'S' shape with rounded legs and back.

3 Travel along your curving 'S' pathway and then hold still. Once again, show me your neat, clear, curving travelling actions. Go!

4 Well done. I liked your curving movements. Now, show me your capital 'I', going straight like a bullet or an arrow to a space near you. You can start low and rise up, soaring like a glider or a bird. You can be wide like a wall with wide spread arms or legs, going sideways. You choose.

5 Ready for your 'I'? Go! And hold your finish, perfectly still.

6 Well done. That was very good and very varied. Now turn, step or jump into your capital 'X'. Which body parts are you crossing? You can be standing, kneeling or lying as you do this.

DANCE - Think of a Number Between 5 and 7 - 13 minutes

1 Find a partner and show each other your three 'S', 'I', 'X' ideas. Partner number one will go first. Ready? Go! Make 'S' and be still. Now make 'I' and be still. Now show your 'X'.

2 Your turn, partner number two. Ready? Go!

3 You and your partner are going to combine and do a 'follow the leader' version of what we have been doing. Discuss, decide and plan your three moves. Partner number one 'the leader' will go first and stop. Partner two follows, copies and stops, and so on, through to a shared way of making your 'X'. Practise freely when you have decided your three actions.

4 Get ready, everyone, for your shared 'S', 'I', 'X' ideas. Number one, go! Number two . . . . follow. Number one . . . . go! Number two . . . . follow. Now your shared 'X', go!

5 Once again, please, but this time you will set your own speeds. Show me your clear starting positions and shapes. Ready? Go!

6 Let's have half the class looking at a demonstration by the other half so that all these excellent ideas, particularly the 'Xs', can be shared. Watch and then tell me which couples you particularly liked and why.

LESSON NOTES AND NC GUIDANCE

Pupils should be taught to:

a *respond readily to instructions.* This is an easy, good fun dance capable of many different levels of outcome, depending on the quality of pupils' attention as they are taken through each of the three stages of the dance. The leader's capital 'S' can be without focus, a nondescript, poor quality movement, followed by an even less impressive partner. Or there can be an eye-catching starting shape, with a part of the body obviously about to lead, neat, wide, curving, travelling actions, clearly led by an arm, shoulder, back, elbow or hip into another eye-catching, clear, still shape.

b *be mindful of others.* As a helpful, co-operative, sympathetic leader it is essential to repeat movements accurately so that your copying partner keeps seeing, for example, the same starting shape, travelling actions and parts leading into the curves. A sequence needs to be repeated for it to be practised, then remembered and presented.

The following, copying partner needs to be equally co-operative, giving his or her whole attention to the leader's actions, to ensure a successful and repeatable performance.

Pupils should be able to show that they can:

a *make simple judgements effectively to improve the accuracy, quality and variety of the performances.* Because the dance is so short, it is easy to arrange demonstrations of the partner work. Half of the class can watch the other half. Pairs can watch pairs. Observers are asked 'Please tell me which pairs you really liked. Tell me what it was that pleased you, so that you might all learn from it, and maybe include it in your own dance.'

Lesson Plan – 30 minutes

Theme:
Christmas and midwinter snow.

WARM-UP ACTIVITIES - 5 minutes

1 In our last lesson we used our bodies to draw the word 'S', 'I', 'X'. Can you now use your bodies in big, lively, warming-up actions to show me the special present you might like for Christmas. I don't want any sitting down, video watching, thank you! Let's pretend there's a prize for the biggest, most physical and imaginative performance. Go!

2 Try to make a repeating pattern. I'll do a golf swing forward; swing back; swing forwards; and drive my golf ball out of sight!

3 Keep working. I see lots of good actions: team games; cycling; flying kites; gliding; canoeing; judo with an imaginary partner.

MOVEMENT SKILLS TRAINING - 17 minutes

Music Sleighride from *Leroy Anderson Favourites* by Saint Louis Symphony Orchestra (2 mins 47 secs)

Time

0 secs All start in a relaxed position, sitting, kneeling or crouching. Ben and Emma will stand until the music starts, then walk about, waving, 'It's snowing. Come out to play.'

12 secs All move round, marvelling at the beautiful snowflakes. Catch them at high, medium and low levels. Rub your hands together or against your clothes. Reach and catch more.

28 secs Make footprints in the snow. Choose to brush the snow gently, flicking it away, or make heavy, deep footprints.

44 secs With your partner, crouch down to make a snowball. Face each other, starting with a small snowball. As it grows, rise up and make it bigger by rolling it sideways.

1 min 3 secs We skate now with the inexpert, awkward number ones going first. You stumble and throw up arms for balance.

1 min 11 secs The expert number twos glide smoothly to all parts of the room – not a stumble anywhere.

1 min 20 secs Inexpert, awkward group, try again. You are worse than ever and some of you even fall down.

1 min 28 secs Expert group, perform even better, sliding gracefully, doing amazing twists and turns, and always in control.

1 min 36 secs Kind experts, pick up your awkward partner, hold on to and lead them through some successful, neat skating.

1 min 45 secs Sleigh arrives with presents for everyone. Catch a parcel, crouch down, unwrap it and then show off what you have received by playing with it. Big, whole body actions, in a repeating, easy to remember sequence, please!

2 mins 20 secs All move into an open circle in pairs behind two leaders and walk round, anti-clockwise.

2 mins 37 secs The line of dancers starts to fall to the floor, with the rear pairs of dancers going down first. The leading pair fall on the last note of music at 2 mins 47 secs.

Well done, everyone. Let's have another practice or two to help you remember all the parts and make them even better.

LESSON NOTES AND NC GUIDANCE

Pupils should be taught to:

a *respond to music.* It helps to speed up the teaching of this dance if pupils are asked to find a partner and sit down near the source of the music. They are told that partner work will take place in two parts of the dance: the making of snowballs and the skating. Partners are asked to number themselves one or two for the skating.

'Listen to the music and I will tell you the actions that accompany each section. Imagine yourselves dancing to each section as I talk you through.' The teacher can also illustrate the different actions within the several parts to help the seated class imagine performing them.

A confident teacher can then talk and lead the class through the dance, accompanied by the music, to give them a feel for the whole dance – its beginning, middle and end. Subsequently, each part of the dance can be taken, planned in greater detail, repeated, improved, developed and remembered.

b *create simple characters and narratives.* We 'create' or express someone or something through movements associated with the person or the object. Children catching snowflakes; making snowballs; tramping in the snow; ice skating; and playing with a favourite toy, are all expressed through whole body movements, inspired by the teacher's asking 'What actions? What body shapes? Where are they doing it? How are they doing it?'

Pupils should be able to show that they can:

a *respond imaginatively to the various challenges.* Almost total imaginative freedom is given to the class as they plan how to tip toe or tramp through the snow; make an ever-increasing snowball; skate; and choose and use their favourite object for the middle part of the lesson. Brilliant, imaginative ideas are, of course, shared with, and often copied by, the observers.

Lesson Plan – 30 minutes

Theme:
Winter.

WARM-UP ACTIVITIES - 5 minutes

1 Let's split the class into two halves. Each half will skip to the folk dance music for eight counts by itself. When not dancing, stand still. Number ones, go! 1, 2, 3, 4, 5, 6, twos get ready. Twos go, 2, 3, 4, 5, 6, 7 and change. Repeat several times.

2 Dancers, time your movements to touch hands with a non-dancer, on counts seven and eight and say 'Go!' to send them off. If you don't receive a hand touch, it doesn't matter. Go!

MOVEMENT SKILLS TRAINING - 13 minutes

1 In our last lesson we thought about winter and its snow. I want us to think, now, about some winter words and how we might express them in movement. Look at the five words on my card and think about three you might choose for your 'Winter Words' dance.

STAMP SHIVER FREEZE SLIP FALL

2 We will take each word in turn and try showing it in action, to make sure you understand it. Let me hear your suggestions for the kind of movement that best shows the meaning of the word.

3 What about 'Stamp'? On the spot or travelling; heavy; firm; quite slow because of heavy footwear; flat-footed; noisy.

4 'Shiver'? Also on the spot or moving; shaking rapidly; whole body huddled in to oneself; twisting.

5 How can we dance 'Freeze'? It can be a winter word about water; a drip becoming an icicle; or it could be the dancer stiffening into a rigid shape.

6 Our inexpert dancers in the 'Snow Dance' slipped and stumbled out of control. 'Slip' can be a long, smooth action or a sudden move to end a dance.

7 'Fall' can also be used to end a dance and is good fun in slow motion as the person or even the snowman melts or tumbles over.

DANCE - Winter Words - 12 minutes

1 You've all had a practice at the five words, showing them in movement. Sit beside your partner and study the list on my card. Decide which three words appeal to both of you the most.

2 Stand and practise your three words by yourself and see what you think is the best and most sensible order in which to perform them.

3 One of you go and collect a piece of percussion, sit down and watch your partner dancing your three words. Dancers, begin.

4 Dancers, sit down beside your partner. Listen to any advice to help you perform better. Then perform again, and your partner will quietly accompany you with the percussion, starting and stopping you, for each action.

5 Well done, dancers. Well done, musicians, with your friendly, helpful comments and your good, quiet accompaniment and timing.

6 Change places and we will repeat all the practising. (Without percussion; advice; repetition with percussion.)

7 Well done, everyone, once again. Now it's time for couples to look at others to see if you can identify the three actions.

LESSON NOTES AND NC GUIDANCE

Pupils should be involved in:

a *the continuous process of planning, performing and evaluating with the greatest emphasis on the performing.* Thinking about any Physical Education lesson in National Curriculum terms, the teacher should consider 'Am I providing opportunities and challenges for the class to plan thoughtfully before performing; perform in a focused, neat, poised way; and reflect on their own and others' performances to influence subsequent planning and performing?' Pupils are continually being challenged to 'Show me how you will move to demonstrate "Shiver". How are you planning to "Freeze"? What sort of "Slip" will I see if I watch you? Please plan thoughtfully, then practise.'

Pupils should be taught to:

a *respond to a range of stimuli, through Dance.* Action words on cards are an excellent stimulus for getting a class moving quickly. When words can also stir the imagination with specific, topical ideas, performing becomes more clearly understood and easily visualised. The eventual dance outcome is for real, not just a piece of 'exploration'.

Partner advice and observation are further stimuli, as is an enthusiastic, encouraging, appreciative teacher.

Lesson Plan – 30 minutes

Theme:
Creative, traditional style folk dance.

WARM-UP ACTIVITIES - 5 minutes

1 Follow your leader, two metres apart, copying the leader's actions. Lead your partner into good spaces and include three or four, neat, quiet, contrasting actions. (Contrast, for example, small walking or running steps, hardly travelling, with a lively skip change of step or polka with good travel; gentle bounces on the spot with lively slipping steps sideways.)

2 Change leaders. New leader, keep the same actions, but try to add a change of direction and body shape somewhere. (For example, small steps, body stretched tall on tip toes; lively, long skipping steps with well bent knees and arms; little bounces turning on the spot; chasse side steps to left and back to right with arms and legs parting wide and closing.)

TEACH ONE COUPLE FIGURES TO BE LINKED CREATIVELY - 15 minutes

Partner on left facing top is A. Partner on right is B. Each figure takes eight bars of the music.

1 Cast off to the side, A turning to the left, B turning to the right, and dance to the bottom for four counts, then turn in, meet, joining hands and dance to top and own places for four.

2 Advance and retire and change places. Partners dance towards each other for two counts, then back for two, then they go forwards again, giving right hands to change places. Now in your partner's place, you usually repeat this figure back to your places, giving left hands to change places. Can any of you suggest a different way to return, still lasting eight counts?

3 Dance round your partner and back. A dances round in front of B and back into place. B repeats round A, back into place. The person being danced round, can you do something on the spot as your partner goes round? For example, setting steps, turn to keep facing partner, or give a helping hand to partner, on count three, round to his or her place.

4 Practise your own eight-count figure that develops from the warm-up activities. For example, include one stationary and one travelling partner; partners parting and closing; or one performing on the spot and one travelling round in a circle.

COUPLES PLAN AND PRACTISE OWN 32-BAR DANCE - 10 minutes

You may include one or two of your own ideas in your four-figure dance. The 'advance and retire', with your own ending, if chosen, will be half of the dance.

PLAN	PRACTISE	DEMONSTRATE	SHARE IDEAS	RECEIVE COMMENTS
PLAN AGAIN	ADAPT	IMPROVE	PRACTISE	REMEMBER

LESSON NOTES AND NC GUIDANCE

Pupils should be taught to:

a *be physically active.* Folk dance lessons should be among the most vigorous and physical because they have a continuous, repeating pattern, maintained by the musical accompaniment. The teacher's responsibility is to give clear, succinct explanations and demonstrations of the new figures or steps, and then let the class practise them.

b *be mindful of others.* 'Others' include other couples sharing the floor space with you, requiring you to restrict yourself to a space, sometimes less than you would like. 'Others' include partners dependent on your being in the right place at the right time (not early or, worse, late) for the successful completion of a figure. Being 'mindful' means that you will work hard, co-operatively and unselfishly with your partner, in deciding on your joint, created dance.

c *perform a number of dances from different times and places, including some traditional dances of the British Isles.* The set and the figures used are typical in English and Scottish country dance.

Pupils should be able to show that they can:

a *repeat sequences with increasing control and accuracy.* Being able to link together a series of movements is an important feature within the National Curriculum. It is easily achieved and practised in a folk dance setting, with the pattern of four repeating figures and the rhythmic musical accompaniment.

Lesson Plan – 30 minutes

Theme:
Traditional folk dance.

WARM-UP ACTIVITIES - 5 minutes

1 Stand with your partner in the A or B groups into which I have divided the class.

2 A group, you will start, travelling together for eight counts. While the As are travelling about the room, the B group will do a partner activity on the spot for eight counts (e.g. turning; advancing and retiring; one dancing on the spot, one dancing round the other; chasse one way for four counts and back for four).

3 Change over the actions for the next eight counts.

4 Continue, alternating travelling with a practice on the spot.

HALF WATCH HALF DEMONSTRATING THEIR TWO SETS OF FIGURES - 4 minutes

1 While you are watching, look out for and tell me which couples kept together, danced neatly and quietly, and were in time with the music at all times.

2 Thank you for your lively demonstrations and your friendly, helpful comments. Let's have another practice and try to use some of the good features that were admired.

TEACH AND DANCE - Farmer's Jig - 15 minutes

Music Farmer's Jig or any 32-bar jig tune.

Formation Longways set of four couples.

Bars 1–8 All couples join nearer hands and walk to top of set for four counts. All turn and return to own places for four counts.
Bars 9–16 All couples join both hands and slip step (quick chasse or gallop) to top of set for four counts. All turn and slip step back to places for four counts.

Bars 17–24 First and second couples dance right and left hand star, while third and fourth couples do the same.
Bars 25–32 All face top of set where first couple cast off, A to the left, B to the right, others following. First couple make an arch at the bottom, others promenade up the centre to re-make set with a new first couple who will repeat the dance.

This can be a folk dance such as 'Cumberland Reel' or 'Djatchko Kolo', or, for variety, a creative dance from a previous lesson, such as 'Snow Dance' or 'Think of a Number Between 5 and 7'.

LESSON NOTES AND NC GUIDANCE

Pupils should be taught to:

a *be physically active.* Vigorous leg activity while travelling is a continuous feature of a folk dance lesson, and the teacher should be aiming to fill the lesson with such action. Praise in the warm-up is for those demonstrating wholehearted and vigorous activity. In the easy dance, all four couples are kept busy throughout.

b *be mindful of others.* The important 'others' here are your partner and the three other couples making the long set with you. To maintain the continuous flow of the dance, all eight must watch what is happening and be ready to start each of the figures at the right time. The teacher should praise and demonstrate with a group 'whose excellent teamwork makes the dance run smoothly, with everyone performing non-stop.'

c *respond to music.* The eight-bar phrasing of the music is practised in the warm-up. The ability to keep in time with the music is praised in the demonstrations. Taking eight counts exactly for each figure of the four figure dance is continually emphasised. This is helped by the teacher's rhythmic accompaniment of the actions and timing of each figure. 'Hands joined, walk to top; turn and back again; . . . .'

d *perform a number of dances from different times and places, including some traditional dances of the British Isles.* This English folk dance is simple and has a repeating pattern of four varied figures. The non-stop action for all four couples makes it a very lively, physical and sociable dance.

Lesson Plan – 30 minutes

Theme:
Circus.

WARM-UP ACTIVITIES - 5 minutes

1 Stand in a big circle, facing the centre, and start straight away with me. Skip to the centre, 3, 4; stay and clap hands for 4; chasse sideways out for 4. In your own starting places, show me a favourite action on the spot. You choose. Go! 1, 2, 3 and stop!

2 Again, and keep to my timing. In to the centre, 3, 4; stay and clap, 3, 4; chasse out, 3, 4; on the spot, you decide. (Keep repeating.)

MOVEMENT SKILLS TRAINING - 15 minutes

1 Still in our circle, face anti-clockwise for the circus parade start to what will be our dance. We parade through town, waving to attract the attention of the townspeople.

2 Within the parade, do one action only, and keep repeating it. Front group, be the band with big drumming or blowing actions. Middle group, juggle with really big arm swings. Those at the back, be clowns with silly walks and throwing pails of water.

3 Well done, paraders. Your big actions were eye-catching. Stand in your sixes now, in the positions where I said you would perform. Each group in turn will work by itself in its own circus ring. All the others gather round the performers quickly to watch them and to react to the skill, fun, excitement or danger. Move fast from ring to ring, spectators, as the performers change.

4 Trapezists, in pairs, swing forwards and back, towards and away from each other, then swing forwards and fly to change trapezes.

5 Clowns, do slapstick, funny walks, punching and missing, and throwing pails of water over the spectators.

6 Jugglers, use a repeating pattern of throwing and catching, for example, in front, to the sides and overhead, up behind the back.

7 Tightrope walkers can balance forwards, forwards, wobble, wobble; balance back, back, wobble, wobble, and keep repeating it.

8 Acrobats, do cartwheels, jumps with a turn, tuck or jacknife, or work with a partner to hold a clever balance.

9 After all the acts by one group, you can do any action of your choice, including one already done such as the band, or a new one such as lion tamer or strong man or woman.

DANCE - Umpteen Rings Circus - 10 minutes

Music *TV Sport* from *Festival of Music* by Central Band of the R.A.F.

40 secs Parade round town
15 secs Trapeze group
17 secs Clowns group
16 secs Jugglers group
19 secs Tightrope walkers group

16 secs Acrobats group
17 secs All do own choice of action
17 secs Re-form circle for parade from town, waving 'Goodbye! We'll see you next year.'

LESSON NOTES AND NC GUIDANCE

Pupils should be taught to:

a *respond to music.* This music is an ideal accompaniment to all parts of the dance – the exuberant march into town; all the larger than life, circus work actions; and the 'See you next year!' waving departure from town.

b *create simple characters and narratives.* We 'create' characters by expressing them through whole body movements normally associated with them. We have to ask 'What are the actions we picture them performing? Where are these actions performed? (e.g. trapezists swinging forwards to a high point; swinging back through a low point to a high). How do they move? (e.g. acrobats with their firm body tension, and beautifully controlled actions; clowns with their floppy, loose, out of control actions).'

Pupils should be able to show that they can:

a *respond imaginatively to the various challenges.* Part of the dance is spent spectating as each group performs. When the dance is over, the teacher can ask 'Please tell me which of the groups really used their imagination and caught your interest.'

b *repeat sequences with increasing control and accuracy.* The greatest aid to remembering and repeating a sequence is a helpful rhythm and a repeating pattern of two, three or four actions.

Lesson Plan – 30 minutes

Theme:
Gestures.

WARM-UP ACTIVITIES - 5 minutes

In much the same way that we paraded, waving, in our 'Circus' dance, I want you to march smartly for eight counts, turn on the spot, march for four counts, then make four quick waves to four different classmates. Do not speak. Let your body gestures speak for you. 'Hello!' 'Hi!' Marching, turning, gesturing, go! March smartly, 3, 4, 5, 6, 7, now turn; turn, 2, 3, 4; wave, 2, 3, 4; march briskly, swing your arms, 5, 6, 7, 8; turn, turn, turn, turn; 'Hello! Hello!', 3, 4; again . . . .

MOVEMENT SKILLS TRAINING - 15 minutes

1 Gesturing is like speaking with your body. Big gestures after a 'Goal!' are seen every week on TV. Use your body to tell me that you or your team have just scored a 'Goal!'

2 Try it on the spot: walk into it, bringing your punching arm from behind to high in front, or do an enormous leap up on the spot.

3 Try one in slow motion now, which probably means a long arm pull from behind with your body rotating into the action.

4 Show me the kind of gesture the goalkeeper might make if poor defending caused the goal. Stamping foot? Clenched fist?

5 Later in the game, the referee refuses all demands by team A for a penalty kick. How will team A and its supporters gesture towards the hated referee? Will they point a finger threateningly? Punch a clenched fist, back and forwards?

6 One team A player is so cheeky towards the referee that he is sent off in disgrace. Show me how the referee and all the team B players might signal 'Off!' to this player who is reluctant to go. Will it be one arm pointing in the direction of the changing rooms? Or a hand on hips, head high, look of disgust?

7 One player, trying to influence the referee, falls down and his or her body is gesturing 'Oooooh! I'm in pain! I was fouled!' How will our crafty actor do this without saying a word?

8 Show me how players in the other team might make a fool of this player, pretending they are all in pain. Show me your body expressing 'Oooooh! Aaaaaa! Agony!'

1 Well done, goal scorers, supporters, referees and wounded. You did say and gesture things to me without saying a word.

2 Find a partner. Decide who will be asking a favour by gesturing to say 'Please!' or 'You must!' or 'I need it!' or 'Please! I'm desperate!' or 'Give it to me, or else!'

3 Decide who will be replying by gestures, saying 'No!' or 'Never!' or 'You're wasting my time!' or 'You must be joking!' or 'Go away!'

4 You can pretend to be two friends, or parent and child. It's going to be a one minute struggle to see who wears out the other person with greater determination. Get started, please.

5 One person can walk away at one point and be pursued and confronted by the other one, pleading. Keep struggling, everyone!

6 Let's look at lots of these gesturing duos, and see who we think are the winners. Look out for any surprising gestures, please.

LESSON NOTES AND NC GUIDANCE

Pupils should be taught to:

a *adopt the best possible posture and use of the body.* If 'gesturing is like speaking with your body' we must try to be eloquent, wholehearted and even larger than life in the way that we use our spine, arms, shoulders and head movements to 'say' something. The focus is on the whole body in movement.

b *express feelings, moods and ideas.* The game provides opportunities to express, by gesture, feelings of joy, disgust, anger, rejection, pain and sarcasm. The partners' dance allows for expressions of pleading and rejection. At all times the expression of the feeling is through the associated movement.

c *create simple characters and stories.* Referee, goalkeeper, angry players, fouled players; and friends, parent or child characters, and their stories, are all expressed and identified through their whole body gestures and actions.

Pupils should be able to show that they can:

a *make simple judgements about their own and others' performances.* Couples can watch couples 'speaking with their bodies' after being asked by the teacher 'Tell me if you think the couple you watch are successful in expressing, through their gestures and body movements, particular feelings or emotions. Tell me also, please, how the expression might be improved.'

Lesson Plan – 30 minutes

Theme:
Traditional folk dance.

WARM-UP ACTIVITIES - 6 minutes

1 Partners are numbered one and two. Number one dances, travelling for eight bars of the music, using their own choice of steps. Number two stays on the spot with small, bouncy steps, claps and gestures in time with the music, and two, watch the action or actions of your partner.

2 Partners, change roles, and new travelling partner two use a different travelling step or steps to those of your partner. Number one, you quietly, easily, move on the spot with upper body and arms moving more than legs. Number one, you also watch your partner's travelling.

3 Partners, decide which of your travelling and on the spot actions and movements you like best and then plan how to use them as you both dance on the spot, one metre apart, then travel separately but identically with eight counts for each. Keep repeating your on the spot and separate travelling actions.

TEACH AND DANCE - Wrona Gapa (Poland) - 18 minutes

Music   Wrona Gapa, Society for International Folk Dancing (cassette 1).

Formation   Couples form a circle, facing partners with the boy on the inside of the circle. Inside hands are held.

Figure A
Bar 1   Starting with the outside foot (boy's left, girl's right), take one step in line of dance, anti-clockwise, close inside foot, step on outside foot.
Bar 2   Hop on the outside foot, swinging inside leg across outside leg; swing back in opposite direction, hopping again on outside foot.
Bars 3–4   Repeat the above in the opposite direction, changing hands and starting on outside foot (boy's right, girl's left).
Bars 5–6   Repeat bars 1–4.

Figure B
Bars 1–8   Ballroom hold; eight polka steps clockwise.
Dance is repeated.

(Ballroom hold. Partners face each other. Boy's right arm is around girl, just below shoulder blade. Boy's left arm is forwards at shoulder height with left hand holding girl's right hand. Girl's left hand is on partner's right shoulder.)

REVISE A FAVOURITE DANCE - 6 minutes

'Wrona Gapa' is a most lively and vigorous dance with both partners performing, non-stop. The final dance should be contrasting and less vigorous, such as a set dance where dancers are involved for only part of the time, or a gentle dance like 'Gestures'.

LESSON NOTES AND NC GUIDANCE

Pupils should be taught to:

a *respond readily to instructions.* In particular, when the steps or figures of a new dance are not easy, everyone in the class must listen and respond sensibly. Otherwise, the dance will keep breaking down because of one or two who don't know where they are going, what they should be doing, or what is coming next.

b *be mindful of others.* Being 'mindful of others', in this case, means paying full attention to what is being explained so that you and your partner will be successful. It also means giving your partner a helping hand, if necessary, and trying to control all your movements.

c *perform a number of dances from different times and places.* This 'different place' dance makes an interesting addition to the class repertoire and is extremely vigorous.

Pupils should be able to show that they can:

a *remember and repeat a series of movements, performed previously.* The ability to repeat, practise, improve, learn and remember previous dances is put to the test when the teacher asks 'Please suggest a favourite dance for us to finish with.' This invitation also gives the teacher the opportunity to see which dances they seem to have remembered with pleasure – an essential element.

Lesson Plan – 30 minutes

Theme:
Creating simple characters.

WARM-UP ACTIVITIES - 5 minutes

1 The chase is an exciting part of crime films. Let me see you dodging away on silent feet. Go!

2 When the drum sounds, freeze! Be still so no-one sees you.

3 Your chaser is nearer now, so tip toe silently from hiding place to hiding place, from alleyways to crouched behind cars.

4 Now, make a break for it with continual right angle turns into passageways and round street corners.

5 Join all the actions together – the quick, silent dodge; the freeze; the slow, silent, tip toes travel; and the desperate dash.

MOVEMENT SKILLS TRAINING - 15 minutes

1 Find a partner and decide who is the cop and who is the robber. Robber, crouch down low, out of sight of the cop who is standing next to you, with his or her back towards you.

2 Robber, silently and slowly, creep away from the policeman.

3 Copper, look to the left and right, twice, while marching on the spot. You frown because you can feel that something is wrong.

4 Policeman, marching with high knee lift, turn round, see burglar and point at him or her.

5 Burglar, aware that you have been seen, start to run, in slow motion.

6 Cop, point at the escaping robber, while marching on the spot, then move in pursuit of the baddie, now running fast on the spot.

7 Both agree a pattern of four chases, ending with policeman grabbing the robber with one arm.

8 Burglar, throw a custard pie at the policeman who falls.

9 Policeman, pick up a custard pie and throw it. Burglar, fall.

10 Cops and robbers, agree your final action. For example, two pies, thrown at same time, and both fall; or 'Gotcha!' as baddie is held; or one creeps away while other samples and eats the pie.

11 Freeze on your end positions.

Music *Easy Winners* from the film *The Sting* by Scott Joplin.

0 secs Starting positions. Robber, crouch down with policeman's back towards you, and unaware of you.

15 secs Burglar, slowly, silently, creep away from the policeman.

25 secs Cop, look to right, left, right and left, very suspicious.

36 secs Cop, slow march on the spot, then turn, see and point at the burglar.

59 secs Burglar, do slow motion running, then faster on spot.

1 min 20 secs Policeman, slow walk on the spot, then move towards the burglar, starting the chase.

1 min 40 secs The chase sequence includes slow motion, or on the spot, or much pointing by the policeman who eventually catches and grabs robber with one hand.

2 mins 10 secs Burglar, throw a custard pie. Policeman, fall down.

2 mins 20 secs Policeman, throw a pie. Burglar, fall down.

2 mins 32 secs Partners, agree final action and freeze in it.

LESSON NOTES AND NC GUIDANCE

Pupils should be taught to:

a *express feelings, moods and ideas.*

b *create simple characters and narratives.* As always, when trying to be 'expressive' and 'creative', it helps to have a specific image so that the class can easily understand where they are and what they are trying to do.

Pupils should be able to show that they can:

a *practise, improve and refine performance.* Questioning by the teacher will help to develop and improve the work. 'What will your starting shape be? Proud, upright, swaggering cop? Curled up, still robber? How will the robber creep away? How will the suspicious cop move to express suspicion? Will your slow motion chase be on the spot or moving, and how will you best show its slow motion character?'

Performance is also improved by demonstrations, followed by comments from the observers. Such comments can include suggestions for improvement.

Lesson Plan – 30 minutes

Theme:
Togetherness.

WARM-UP ACTIVITIES - 5 minutes

1 Find a partner. Face each other with one hand joined. Number one will dance in a circle round two who turns on the spot. Eight counts.

2 Number two dances in a circle round one who remains, turning, on the spot, with one hand joined. Eight counts.

3 Partners skip together, nearer hands joined, for six counts, then meet with and stand facing another couple, on counts seven and eight.

4 Two counts to each movement, couples reach in and touch right hands at head height, then lower; left hands in, touch and lower; both hands in, touch and lower; all join hands lightly.

5 Couples separate and start again, hands joined, one on spot, one circling round.

MOVEMENT SKILLS TRAINING - 15 minutes

1 Before we make our class machine dance all joined together, let's practise some machine-like ways of moving. Show me pushing down actions, like corks into bottles, on the spot or turning, or moving along an assembly line. Pushing down . . . . go!

2 Are you using one hand at a time, or both at the same time? What sort of sounds will accompany your firm pushing? A sudden blowing out of breath; a grunt; 'poom, poom, poom'?

3 A piston action pushes forwards and back. Try this with arms bending and stretching as if you are turning the wheels of a train. Use both arms, one going forwards as one comes back. What kind of whirring, turning sounds will you use?

4 A grabbing machine lifts something up from a passing assembly line, and places it down somewhere else – maybe tins to be packaged. Show me how this might happen. A body turn to place it would be interesting. Reach; lift; twist; place. 'Choong! Boomp!'

5 Another kind of grabbing machine can dig down, scoop and throw. Are you throwing to left, right or overhead? 'Scoop! Whoosh!'

6 Try an action and reaction. For example, both arms stretched forwards. One arm is still until the other hand strikes it to turn your body through 90 degrees. Or one hand presses down on your head to make your body bend. Other hand strikes under your seat to rise again.

DANCE - Our Class Machine - 10 minutes

1 Walk in and out of one another, thinking about your favourite kinds of machine action. When I call 'Stop!' be still.

2 Stop! Be still, like switched-off machines. Chris, at the centre of the class, please start your machine-like movement, with, I hope, some interesting voice sounds.

3 One by one, starting with those nearest to Chris and the centre, move in to link with the machine that started ahead of you.

4 Please try to make our machine interesting with no two linked actions the same. A contrasting set of voice sounds would also be very welcome.

5 Rest for a moment, everyone, and stay in your positions. Can you possibly improve the whole machine's variety by moving more up and down, around, along a short assembly line – or by a brilliant voice sound accompaniment?

LESSON NOTES AND NC GUIDANCE

Physical Education should involve pupils in:

a *the continuous process of planning, performing and reflecting, with the greatest emphasis on the actual performance.* For any teacher interested in reflecting on his or her lesson, there are three important post-lesson questions in terms of the National Curriculum.

1 Did I provide opportunities, and challenge the pupils to plan ahead, thoughtfully? Without such planning, there is no focus or thought behind the participation. 'Can you plan . . . . ?'; 'Can you show me . . . . ?'; and 'Show me how . . . .' are questions used to inspire the specific thinking ahead that justifies our calling the lesson 'educational'.

2 Was the time allocated for performing adequate? Was there an impression that the lesson was a 'scene of busy activity with everyone working, almost non-stop?'

In their performances, did the pupils display quiet, neat, well-controlled work; vigour and poise with some originality; variety and contrast; and the ability to make it all look 'easy'?

3 Were there moments in the lesson when a demonstration was organised and observers were asked to reflect on 'correctness', quality, the main features, what was liked and worth copying, and any ways in which it might be improved? Because they are time-consuming, demonstrations with follow-up comments should only happen once or twice in the lesson.

Lesson Plan – 30 minutes

Theme:
Basic actions of travelling, jumping, turning.

WARM-UP ACTIVITIES - 5 minutes

1 Step forwards for three counts and bring feet together on four. Forwards, 2, 3, feet together. Walk backwards for three counts and bring feet together on four. Back, 2, 3, feet together.

2 Again. Forwards, 2, 3, together; back, 2, 3, together; step, 2, 3, feet together; back, 2, 3 and stop!

3 Well done. Now add four sideways stepping movements, starting to the left. It's called a chasse as we step left; close right to left; step left; and close right to left.

4 Now to the right. Step right, close left; step right; close left. To both sides. Left, close; left, close; right close; right, together.

5 Practise your steppings and feet closings to this lively music. Add in a two-beat pause before changes of direction if you want.

MOVEMENT SKILLS TRAINING - 15 minutes

1 Can you plan your own pattern? Decide on the number of steps in each direction, with or without pauses.

2 Add in one jump somewhere. Where will it be? At the start or finish? To change direction? Within your stepping? You choose, then keep practising your whole pattern.

3 Now add a spin. Keep the present pattern going. Keep your newly added jump, and somewhere add a spin, small or large.

4 A long, slow spin will be easier to follow. Is your hand, arm or shoulder leading you round into your turn? Make it obvious.

5 Make your stepping, jumping, turning into a repeating, flowing pattern – always in time with the music.

6 Find a partner and show each other your pattern.

DANCE - Stepping, Jumping, Spinning, Gesturing - 10 minutes

1 With your partner, decide how you will combine your actions so that you are both represented in a steps, jump and spin dance.

2 As you dance together, are you following a leader; facing each other; side by side; or going away from each other and coming back again?

3 Finally, to complete your partners dance sequence, can you add a gesture – of triumph, success, pride, pleasure, or whatever, to make me have a special look at your pair?

4 Your gesture can be anywhere. At the start, it can be a way of gathering for 'Let's go!' At the end it can be a way of saying 'We're brilliant, aren't we!'

5 Pairs, always look for good spaces as you practise, repeat, improve and remember all of your:

    stepping jumping spinning gesturing

6 Let's have each half of the class looking at and commenting on the other half. Look out for and tell me about the partners and their actions that you particularly liked. I might also ask you to suggest something helpful to make a performance even more admirable.

LESSON NOTES AND NC GUIDANCE

Pupils should be taught to:

a *recognise the safety risks of wearing inappropriate clothing, footwear and jewellery.*

b *respond readily to instructions.*

c *be mindful of others.* The setting of standards and an explanation of what is, and is not acceptable, should take place during the first lessons of a new school year. This becomes increasingly necessary as pupils become older. This NC requirement is concerned with the way pupils dress, listen, behave, work and show a regard for others sharing the space and working with them.

    Badly-dressed classes wear jewellery, e.g. watches, rings, necklaces; large, fashionable, ungiving, noisy 'trainers'; long trousers or leg coverings that catch heels; too many layers of clothing; the clothes they wore to school; long hair that is unbunched and impedes vision.

    Badly-behaved classes contain some who talk incessantly; do not listen to or respond to the teacher; need instructions repeated time after time; do not start or stop when told to; disturb and upset others by their selfish, noisy, unsafe rushing around; and work at a pitifully low, half-hearted level, destroying lesson enjoyment for the majority of pupils and the teacher.

    A safe environment requires a well-dressed, well-behaved, quiet, attentive and responsive class. Good behaviour must be pursued continually until it becomes the normal, expected way to work. There is nothing to talk about, apart from those occasions when comments are asked for, usually after a demonstration, or when partners are quietly discussing their response to a challenge.

Lesson Plan – 30 minutes

Theme:
Contrasting actions.

WARM-UP ACTIVITIES - 5 minutes

1 Tip toe silently, pretending someone is asleep and you must not waken them. Tiny, little, gentle steps. Shhhhh!

2 Pretend the floor is a drum now, and you want your loud, heavy beating to be heard above all the others. Go! Bang! Bang! Bang!

3 Travel with your feet never leaving the floor as you slide, slither and glide along the surface of the floor making very little sound. Slowly, softly, skim along the surface of the floor.

4 Now the floor is red hot and you leap and bound to keep high above it. Bounce and bounce and leap up high.

MOVEMENT SKILLS TRAINING - 12 minutes

1 In addition to the gentle and strong, light and heavy contrasts we have practised, we can use fast and slow, and direction change contrasts. Think of a favourite travelling action, using your feet.

2 As I call out 'Normal!' or 'Slow motion!' or 'Fast forwards!' or 'Direction!', can you change the speed or direction of your action? Ready? Normal . . . . fast forwards . . . . slow motion . . . . normal . . . . direction . . . . fast forwards . . . . normal . . . . slow motion . . . . directions . . . . stop!

3 Well done. Your responses were immediate and very contrasting.

4 Can you make a pattern with two pairs of opposites? Aim for variety as well as contrast. For example, can your changes include actions, body shape, direction, speed or force?

5 The medium-speed, rhythmic music is quick enough for stepping and travelling, but slow enough for turns, gestures and big body movements with its 1, 2, 3, 4; opposite, 2, 3, 4 rhythm. Begin.

1 Well done. I saw many good examples of 'Opposites'. Find a partner and take turns at showing each other your four-part sequence with its two pairs of opposites.

2 Partners, can you now plan a four-part sequence, using the best of your two routines, ideally with a good and varied mixture?

3 Keep practising and chant out the nature of your opposites. For example, 'Slow and soft, on the spot; quick and strong, travelling; rise and open, 3, 4; lower and close, 3, 4.'

4 If you prefer, you can repeat each half of your pattern to make your sequence last longer.

5 Finally, decide if you will perform the movements together; or have one do the first movement alone with the other showing the opposite and contrasting movement alone. Working alone can be interesting with one on the spot, the other travelling around the stationary one. In rising and falling, for example, you would be holding opposite shapes at the end.

6 Let's have each half watching the other half to look out for and identify imaginative ideas and neat performances.

7 Thank you for your varied and interesting demonstrations and your friendly, helpful comments. Let's have more practice so that you can include any of the good ideas seen and praised to help improve your performances.

LESSON NOTES AND NC GUIDANCE

Pupils should be taught to:

a *be physically active.* Good dress, good behaviour, an instant response to instructions, an unselfish sharing of floor space, and consideration for others are the initial priorities to be pursued with a new class.

The next priority is to make the lessons physically demanding, with pupils working wholeheartedly and almost non-stop. There is a world of difference between a half-hearted, undemanding way of working and a vigorous, energetic, whole body involvement, using joints and muscles to their maximum potential.

b *compose and control their movements by varying shape, size, level, direction, speed and tension.* Many times during their Dance lessons the teacher will have told the class that variety and contrast within a performance enhance and improve the appeal of the performance. An 'Opposites' dance reminds them of examples of variety and contrast within movement.

Pupils should be able to show that they can:

a *respond imaginatively to the various challenges.* The challenge to 'Plan a four-part sequence with two pairs of "opposites"' is pupil-centred, with ample opportunity to be original, creative and highly imaginative. The challenge for the teacher is to see good examples of such imaginative creativity, and to share it with the class.

Lesson Plan – 30 minutes

Theme:
Patterns.

WARM-UP ACTIVITIES - 5 minutes

1 Let's all clap to this folk dance music and feel its eight-count phrasing. Clap, 2, 3, 4, 5, 6, 7, repeat.

2 Let me clap the first four beats and you do the last four in each phrase. Ready? Me, 2, 3, 4; you, 2, 3, 4; me, 2, 3, 4; you, 2, 3, stop!

3 Now do eight travelling steps, keeping with the music's rhythm. Travel, 2, 3, 4, 5, 6, 7, again. Travel, 2, 3, 4, 5, 6, 7, again.

4 Travel again, but be still on four of the eight beats. Then listen very carefully to the beat to join back in again. It could be 'Still, still, 3, 4; travel, travel, 3, 4', or 'Travel, 2, 3, 4; still, 2, 3, 4'. You decide where your 'action gaps' will be. Begin!

MOVEMENT SKILLS TRAINING - 15 minutes

1 Let's try a pattern of eight claps on the spot with little leg action (for example, little bounces in knees); then an eight-count travelling; then clapping on the spot; then travelling.

2 Try an 'action gap' on four of the claps, and four of the travelling steps. Listen carefully, counting to yourself, to join in again.

3 Good. Most of you kept in time, counting through the gaps.

4 On the spot, this time, pretend the floor is a drum as you make rhythmic sounds with your lively feet – bouncing, stamping, jumping, hopping or running. You can clap, also, if you wish.

5 Travel for eight counts in a way that contrasts with your earlier travelling. For example, tiny, long or wide steps; more gentle or more vigorous; fast or slow; sideways or backwards; curving round in a circle instead of straight.

6 Now for our four-part pattern – clapping on the spot with little leg action; travelling; lively feet on the spot; travel to show a contrast with previous travel. Get ready. Begin.

DANCE - Partners and Patterns - 10 minutes

1 Find a partner and show each other your four-part, repeating pattern. While you are watching, count to eight to check that your partner is exactly in time with each phrase of the music.

2 Plan to combine two of your own and two of your partner's actions to make your shared pattern. Practise until you can remember and repeat it. Quietly clap, 3, 4, 5, 6, now you travel; travel, 2, 3, 4, 5, 6, now on the spot; lively feet, 3, 4, 5, 6, 7, 8; different travel, different travel, 5, 6, 7, repeat.

3 Well done. I saw lots of interesting variety. Variety also comes from the ways that you work as a pair. You can have one on the spot and one travelling during each phrase of the music. You can face each other on the spot, then travel, side by side; or follow a leader; or part and close. Discuss, decide, practise please.

4 Well done. Can each of you now include one four-count stillness? Where will you do this? At the start, finish or in the middle? Both in the same place or not? Where do you think it will be most dramatic to hold a pause and an interesting body shape?

5 Let's see if you can keep in time with the music, without my counting, as you keep repeating your four-part pattern. We can then have a look at couples still in time with the music at the end.

LESSON NOTES AND NC GUIDANCE

Pupils should be taught to:

a *be mindful of others.* The 'others', in this case, include the remainder of the class with whom you are sharing the floor space. It might be necessary to practise travelling 'along straight lines, never following another' as you visit all parts of the room – the ends, sides and corners as well as the middle. Most primary school children will travel, anti-clockwise, in a big circle, if not taught otherwise.

'Others' also include your partner with whom you are combining unselfishly and co-operatively, listening to and acting upon his or her views for the benefit of the partner work.

Pupils should be able to show that they can:

a *repeat sequences with increasing control and accuracy.* The ability to plan, practise, improve, learn, remember and repeat a sequence of movements is a main target within the NC. Having a repetitive, rhythmic pattern of two, three or four actions is a great aid to remembering and repeating. When the teacher is able to rhythmically accompany the actions, this helps the partners to keep with the music, and acts as a reminder of what is happening and what comes next. 'Clap on the spot, 3, 4, 5, 6, now we travel; travel, travel, off you go, 5, 6, now on the spot; lively, lively, on the spot, 5, 6, travel again; new action, travel, travel, 5, 6, 7, stop!'

Lesson Plan – 30 minutes

Theme:
Action words with percussion accompaniment.

WARM-UP ACTIVITIES - 5 minutes

1 An earlier lesson was about contrasting movements. The way I sound my tambourine will tell you how I want you to move. Can you recognise and respond to slow or quick; quiet or loud; soft or vigorous; big or little; even happy or sad? Ready? Go!

2 Good. I liked your speedy responses to my changing rhythms.

3 Show me your movements to my loud banging alternating with my gentle tapping. Space out well and visit all parts of the room.

4 Now show me your actions to my shaking alternating with my smooth rubbing of the tambourine.

MOVEMENT SKILLS TRAINING - 15 minutes

1 All show me a travelling action to my tambourine accompaniment. When I stop playing, be perfectly still. When I re-start, travel again. Listen for my silences! Go!

2 Please find a partner. One of you collect a piece of percussion. The other collect one set of three cards and place them down on the floor in front of you in their numbered order, 1, 2, then 3. Study the words and plan how you will dance the actions.

3 Dancers, stand ready to perform your three actions on your little stage. Partners, watch carefully so that you can make helpful comments. Without percussion at this stage, start when you are ready.

4 Well done, dancers. Now sit down and be given some friendly, helpful advice to improve your performance. Were the actions clear? Were the body shapes full and clear? Was the timing good or was it too rushed, or too long? Partners, tell them what was good, but also tell them how to improve.

5 The same dancers again, please. Partners with percussion, you may quietly accompany your partner, starting and stopping to make the three actions distinct and separate. Begin when ready.

6 Well done, everyone. The improvements were obvious. Let's have one more practice, then we'll change places, dancers and percussionists.

DANCE - Pairs with Percussion - 10 minutes

1 All hide the words on your cards now and sit beside another couple who do not know what your three actions are. Each couple has a turn at presenting their dance and the watching couple have to try to identify the three actions being performed. Both partners can have a turn as dancer and as percussionist to give the observers a second look.

2 Percussionists, remember to stop and start each action to keep them separate. Play quietly so that you do not disturb other couples. First couples, please begin.

3 Well done, first couples. I am pleased to hear that most of the watchers were able to recognise and name your three actions. Now change places, please, and start again.

4 Well done, second couples, and very observant watchers.

5 Now I will choose some couples. Can you recognise their actions?

ACTION WORDS ON CARDS FOR 'PAIRS WITH PERCUSSION' DANCE

There are three sets of numbered cards, each of which has the number 1, 2 or 3, and one word on it. It helps in re-grouping the cards after the lesson if each numbered set of cards is a different colour – blue for 1s, green for 2s and yellow for 3s, for example.

The cards numbered 1 have an action word for the first part of the dance – the travelling on to each couple's little 'stage'. The cards numbered 2 have an action word for the middle part of the dance – often performed, with minimum travel, on the stage. The cards numbered 3 have the action word for the final part of the dance – the still, finishing position and shape.

Dancers are asked to 'Show me your starting shape and position which, ideally, will give me some idea of what your first action will be like.' A starting shape for 'creep' will be different to a starting position for 'hurry', for example.

Set 1

LEAP	DRIFT	RUSH	SLITHER	CRAWL
BOUNCE	SKIP	GLIDE	SHOOT	FLY
FLOAT	DART	SLIDE	SWOOP	TROT
DASH	ZOOM	TWIRL	GALLOP	RACE
CREEP	HURRY	SHUFFLE	ZIG-ZAG	CHASE

Set 2

GROW	GESTURE	CIRCLE	STRETCH	TWIST
SPIN	OPEN	HOVER	STAGGER	LEAN
TURN	SIZZLE	SOAR	SWAY	STAMP
BEND	LUNGE	BOUNCE	SHRIVEL	WOBBLE
RISE	CLOSE	SHRINK	WHIRL	WEAVE

Set 3

FREEZE	STRETCH	MELT	COLLAPSE	SHUFFLE
FADE	BURST	FLOW	WHOOSH	TRICKLE
SAG	FALL	FLOP	SINK	FLUTTER
SPIN	SPREAD	SCATTER	EXPLODE	SHRIVEL
DROP	FOLD	CRUMBLE	CURL	TUMBLE

LESSON NOTES AND NC GUIDANCE

Pupils should be taught to:

a *respond readily to instructions.* There are a lot of helpful instructions in the teaching and development of this dance. At each stage, the dancer and the musician must listen carefully as the little dance grows from teacher-led, with no percussion, to the final, percussion-led version.

Pupils should be taught to:

a *respond to a range of stimuli, through Dance.* There is a triple stimulus here. The words provide the movement content; the partner comments, half-way through the development, provide a quality stimulus; the percussion provides the rhythm.

Lesson Plan – 30 minutes

Theme:
Storytelling.

WARM-UP ACTIVITIES - 5 minutes

1 Pretend you are 'winter-sunning' in the sea on some tropical island – well away from our miserable December weather. Show me two or three swimming actions to this slow music. Off you go.

2 Walk, showing me your graceful, relaxed swimming strokes. Your expression will be 'This is the life!'

3 Share the 'water space' sensibly, slowly turning arms in front, back or to the side. It's all very pleasant and peaceful as you weave in and out of each other.

4 If you are swimming backwards, look over one shoulder from time to time.

5 With arms out sideways and small steps on the spot, can you tread water and bob up and down?

6 By lifting your arms straight up above your head, you will sink down, with a bending of your knees. Then push off from the bottom and swim slowly to the surface.

7 Make a little repeating pattern. It could be breast stroke; tread water; sink; push up and back stroke. You decide, then practise it.

MOVEMENT SKILLS TRAINING - 15 minutes

1 At the start of our 'Jaws' dance, the shark is lurking in the corner of the room, crouched low to the floor, in a long shape with arms reaching along the floor, legs stretched out to the rear. Our two sharks, Sue and Tony, can practise from the same corner to start with, and I can help them with their moves.

2 The rest of the class, in the opposite corner, are swimming, completely unaware of the danger. Sharks, look at them, but do not move yet.

3 Sharks, rise slowly. Keep low and creep towards the centre of the room, looking at the swimmers, weaving in and out of one another.

4 Sharks, swim from side to side at the centre of the room, still a good distance away. Some of you swimmers see the threat and your movements become slightly agitated and quicker.

5 Sharks, move away again towards your starting corner, turn and move right down the room, nearly at the swimmers, now reacting and moving anxiously in the corner.

6 Sharks, move from side to side, then close in and circle right round the group in the corner, and finish at the front again.

7 Swimmers, you are now anxious, expressing your fear in rapid arm and shoulder gestures, swimming out of the way in panic.

Music The Water Kite sequence from **Jaws** by John Williams (1 min 30 secs).
Group dance with two groups, one at each end of the hall. Each group contains 'Jaws', and several swimmers.

Time

0 secs 'Jaws', hide low in your corner. Swimmers, enjoy the sea.

20 secs 'Jaws', rise, approach the group, then return almost to your corner.

30 secs 'Jaws', advance half way to the swimmers. Swimmers, some of you become frightened and start to panic.

40 secs Sharks, rush from side to side, trapping swimmers in the corner, then completely encircle the swimmers.

1 min 10 secs Sharks, rush in and grab one of the swimmers who falls to the floor, trying to resist. 'Jaws', grip your swimmer victim, side on by an arm and a leg, and drag him or her, slowly, along the floor, away from the rest of the swimmers, diagonally towards the centre of the room. Remainder of swimmers, crouch low, with both arms reaching forwards and up towards the receding swimmer, expressing your fear and your feeling of helplessness.

1 min 30 secs 'Jaws', complete the pull on your victim at the centre of the hall and the dance ends on the last note of music with the shark, the victim and the swimmer on a diagonal line across your half of the room. The shark's back is towards the centre with both arms stretched towards and holding the victim.

Victim, you are lying, held by 'Jaws', on the same diagonal line. Group of swimmers, low and long stretched, form a close group, facing and still reaching up and out towards the victim.

J = Jaws
V = Victims
S = Swimmers

```
        J              SSS
        V              SSS
                       SSS
      S                 SS
      SS                 S
    SSS
    SSS                 V
    SSS                 J
```

LESSON NOTES AND NC GUIDANCE

Pupils should be able to:

a *create simple characters and stories.*

b *express feelings, moods and ideas.* Creating characters and expressing feelings is easier if there is a clearly understood, easily visualised setting in which the characters and expressions are happening. An isolated 'Can you show me how to express fear?' does not conjure up a helpful image that can be translated into something specific.

Pupils should be able to show that they can:

a *plan imaginatively, perform to convey ideas, and reflect on the performance and suggest ways to improve it.*

Lesson Plan – 30 minutes

Theme:
Winter words and group activity.

WARM-UP ACTIVITIES - 5 minutes

1 This slow, gentle music makes me think of bubbles or balloons flying. Show me how you might choose to move on the spot in response to the music.

2 As you twist and turn, do you feel high, balancing on tip toes? 'Hovering lightly' might describe your floating movements.

3 Travel now, drifting lightly and slowly from space to space. You have no weight and the air carries you, up and down, round and round, sometimes curving, sometimes on straight lines as you weave in and out of one another, like a snowflake.

MOVEMENT SKILLS TRAINING - 15 minutes

1 Join together in groups of five. Make a circle shape and show me your own starting shape as you represent a falling snowflake. Turn on the spot on tip toes, held in space.

2 Can you travel, in and out of one another, close but not touching as you swirl, hover, float, curving and gliding – like a snowflake in the winter wind?

3 Well done, weightless dancers. Now relax and discuss how your three-part pattern will end. Will you make a frozen shape suddenly?; all drop, gently together?; scatter away to land at different places?; or join together to make a beautiful snowflake shape? When you are ready, practise.

4 Let's try your three-part pattern now. Ready? Lightly on the spot, high and weightless; travel, in and out, floating, twisting and turning. Now your own finish, please.

5 Very well done, with many attractive finishes. Let's look at two groups at a time and comment on the ideas and actions that we liked, and any impressions of good 'group togetherness'.

1 Stay in your groups of five and I will give each group a card. Every card has the word 'Scatter' on it, but there are four different versions of how snowflakes scatter for you to plan and perform as a group. Please do not look at another group's card. Later on, you will be guessing what their words are.

2 Continue practising and I will come round and help you to make your movements clearer. Show me your group's clear, still start and finish positions and shapes. Make your actions neat and try to show the particular movement qualities on your card.

SCATTER	SLOWLY	WITH SAME ACTION	VARIED SHAPES ENDING
SCATTER	SWIRLING	ONE AFTER THE OTHER	TO SETTLE
SCATTER	DRIFTING	WITH CHANGES OF SPEED	TO RE-FORM
SCATTER	FLUTTERING	LIGHTLY	SINKING/FREEZING

3 Practise your four-part pattern further. Then we will look at each group in turn to make friendly, helpful comments.

LESSON NOTES AND NC GUIDANCE

Pupils should be taught to:

a *adopt the best possible posture and use of the body.* Often in Dance, the focus is on the travelling actions used to transport us. This is particularly true in folk dance, for example. For variety and to promote well-controlled, poised and versatile whole body movement, we sometimes focus on movements involving the spine, arms and shoulders as well as the legs, as we bend, stretch, twist, turn, curl or arch, expressing movement qualities such as lightness, changing shapes or speed, gentle falling, or a hardening of body tension.

b *compose and control their movements by varying shape, size, level, direction, speed or tension.* After the question 'What action?', we develop by asking 'What shape?', 'Where is the action happening?' and 'How is the action being performed?', to allow consideration for shape, size, level, direction, speed or tension.

Pupils should be able to show that they can:

a *use simple judgements to improve the accuracy, quality and variety of their own performances.* Within the dual emphasis on performing and learning which is the basis of NC Physical Education, reflection and evaluation by pupils helps them to adapt, change and plan again, guided by their own and others' judgements.

Lesson Plan – 30 minutes

Theme:
Traditional, folk dance style, creative dance.

WARM-UP ACTIVITIES - 5 minutes

1 Skip freely by yourself, to visit all parts of the room.

2 Travel along straight lines, not curving round, following others.

3 When drum sounds twice, join with the nearest person and dance.

4 When drum sounds once, separate and dance by yourself.

5 When drum sounds twice, find a different partner to the one you had last time.

FIGURES WHICH CAN BE USED IN A CIRCLE FORMATION - 15 minutes

Each figure takes eight counts of the music. Partners are all in one big circle where they can see the teacher and do easily supervised practice together. A boy dances on the left of the pair.

1 All walk into the centre and out again.

2 Boys alone skip into the centre, then out again.

3 Girls dance into the centre and out again.

4 Chasse with partner, hands joined, into the centre and out again. (Step sideways to centre with nearer foot; close other foot to first foot; step sideways to centre; close other foot. Side, close; side, close; 3 and 4. Step out, close; out, close; 3; and 4.)

5 Join hands in a circle and slip to left and back to right.

6 Perform a Grand Chain, giving alternate hands to the person coming towards you. (Boys travel anti-clockwise, all giving right hands to the first person met.)

7 Promenade, side by side, nearer hands joined, anti-clockwise round in a big circle.

CIRCLES OF FOUR COUPLES PLAN AND PRACTISE OWN DANCE - 10 minutes

1 Each couple chooses to include one of the seven figures opposite. Try to make your dance interesting with variety and contrast – all dancing, then only a few; movements into the circle and out, as well as around in a circle; movements forwards and/or backwards and/or sideways, for example. Each make your choice and practise.

2 Remember there are eight counts to each figure in your four-figure folk dance. Get into the habit of counting in groups of eight.

3 Let us look at each circle in turn. Please look out for and tell me which circle linked its actions smoothly together and included interesting variety and contrast.

4 Thank you, performers and those making helpful comments. Before we continue practising for improvement, can you think of any features of folk dance that improve its appearance?

5 Yes, circles that stay round; neat footwork, always in time with the music, never late or early; good teamwork and being ready to come in at the right time and place; and a general impression of enthusiasm and enjoyment.

LESSON NOTES AND NC GUIDANCE

Pupils should be taught to:

a *be physically active.* One of the best ways to ensure that pupils are almost non-stop physically active is through folk dance lessons. The music provides the continuous accompaniment; the steps and figures are lively; and for most of the dances, all couples in the circle are dancing.

b *be mindful of others.* Being 'mindful of others' means sensibly and unselfishly sharing space when practising, and co-operating considerately in agreeing and planning the four figure repeating pattern of the created dance.

c *perform a number of dances from different times and places, including some traditional dances of the British Isles.* The seven figures taught are typical patterns from English and Scottish country dance. The music is traditional. The emphasis on partners working together, thoughtfully and carefully as part of a larger team, is typical of traditional dance.

d *repeat sequences with increasing control and accuracy.* The repeating pattern of four figures is helped by the teacher counting out the eight-bar phrases of the music for each part, and by the whole class thinking ahead and remembering what comes next. Increasing accuracy depends on the teacher asking for one element to be focused on, and improved, each time.

Lesson Plan – 30 minutes

Theme:
Traditional folk dance.

WARM-UP ACTIVITIES - 5 minutes

Partners in a big circle, all face anti-clockwise, right hands joined, boys on the inside.

1 Do eight skipping steps forwards, side by side, in the circle.

2 Face your partner and, without contact, do four setting steps. (Step to side; close other foot to first foot; mark time on the spot with first foot. Step, close, beat. To side, close, beat. Later a jump is added to the first step. Jump, 2, 3; jump, mark time; side, 2, 3.)

3 Change places with partner, giving right hands for four counts.

4 Face partner and do four setting steps. (Right, 2, 3; left, 2, 3; right, 2, 3; left, 2, 3.)

5 Change back to own places, giving left hands for four counts.

6 Eight skipping steps round, side by side, right hands joined, anti-clockwise in the circle.

Keep repeating.

TEACH AND DANCE - Three Meet (An English Folk Dance) - 18 minutes

Music *Three Meet* by Blue Mountain Band (EFDS), from *Community Dances Manual 1*, or any 32-bar reel tune.

The grand circle round the room is made of trios facing trios. A boy with a partner on each hand faces a girl with a partner on each hand.

Bars 1–8 Trios, advance to meet and retire. Then, still facing the other trio, change places, dropping hands to pass one another.

Bars 9–16 Repeat the advancing and retiring, and the passing to change places, back to original places.

Bars 17–24 All six join hands in a ring and circle to the left, then change direction and circle back, right, to places.

Bars 25–32 Each trio should form a ring, circle left and as the two rings circle, pass each other by revolving round each other and so progress on one place in the grand circle.

Each line of three dancers now opens up to face a new trio to repeat the dance.

REVISE A FAVOURITE DANCE - 7 minutes

This can be a folk dance such as 'Cumberland Reel', 'Djatchko Kolo', 'Farmer's Jig' or 'Wrona Gapa' from previous lessons, or, for variety, a creative dance learned and remembered earlier in the school year. Such a dance, using more modern music or no music, and involving the class in movements different to the traditional steps and patterns opposite, will produce the interesting and varied content that makes a lesson satisfying for everyone.

LESSON NOTES AND NC GUIDANCE

Pupils should be taught to:

a *be physically active and engage in activities that develop the heart and lungs.* Near non-stop, vigorous action is a general feature of folk dance lessons. Continuous use of the big leg muscles inspires healthy development of the heart and lungs – body parts, according to the experts, seldom used for prolonged periods in the modern, mostly sedentary, youngster.

b *perform a number of dances from different times and places, including some traditional dances of the British Isles.* 'Three Meet' is a popular English folk dance, often included to give interesting variety to a dance programme. Unusually, it is made up of trios facing trios in a big circle, all round the room. It is, equally unusually, a progressive dance with all trios, facing anti-clockwise or clockwise, moving on one place in that direction after each completion of the dance, to meet and dance with a new trio.

Pupils should be able to show that they can:

a *repeat a series of movements, performed previously.* By now, the extensive class repertoire should mean that the teacher will receive an encouraging response to the question 'Which favourite dance shall we end the lesson with?' One of the many attractions of folk dances is that they have a long 'shelf life' and pupils are happy to repeat them.

Lesson Plan – 30 minutes

Theme:
Contrasts in movement.

WARM-UP ACTIVITIES - 5 minutes

1 Showing 'contrasts' in our movements means showing clearly how they are different. One obvious contrast is travelling and being still. Please show me an example, from a still starting position.

2 Good. Same again, but with this half of the room showing soft, gentle, travelling into a slow, graceful stop, while the other half vigorously, firmly travel into a sudden, rigid stop. Go!

3 Very good and very contrasting. This time, the silent, graceful half will move slowly through only a short distance travel and finish in a small, 'easy', body shape. The vigorous, lively half will travel far and finish in a wide, firm body shape. Go!

MOVEMENT SKILLS TRAINING - 10 minutes

1 Find a partner and we'll play at 'Anything you can do, we can do different!' Partner A, on the spot, show an action your hands can do. Partner B, join in with an action that demonstrates a contrast. It might be clapping, then fingers bending and stretching. Hands only . . . . go! Keep repeating.

2 Well done, partners B. Now you go first, using feet only, on the spot, challenging your partner to do one that contrasts. For example, lightly peeling feet up from floor and loudly stamping feet down on to floor. Feet only . . . . go! Keep repeating.

3 I saw lots of good contrasts. Partners A, can you show B a whole body movement, on the spot, for them to contrast?

4 Let's look at some excellent contrasts: rise, fall; open, close; stretch, curl; shake loosely, turn stiffly; and flop, freeze.

1 Stay with your partner and find a couple to work with. Couple A will plan travelling actions to a still finish. Couple B will plan whole body movements on the spot.

2 With your own partner, discuss, plan and practise your actions or movements, to show to the other couple.

3 Find a good starting place, pairs of couples, for A to show their travelling actions, then be still. Bs watch, discuss, then follow with contrasting travelling actions. Keep practising your actions which can include contrasting, still starting and finishing shapes.

4 Excellent. Your groups of four are now working and contrasting well together.

5 B couples, show the other couples your big body movements on the spot. Decide how often you will repeat them before becoming still to wait for the As to discuss and decide how they will contrast with you.

6 Well done, with lots of contrasting actions, shapes, levels and groupings. Now, show me your group starting positions for your whole pattern of contrasting travelling and actions on the spot. Keep going. Go!

7 While each half of the class perform for the other half, those watching, please look out for good examples of contrasts and be able to describe the differences, so that we can all learn.

LESSON NOTES AND NC GUIDANCE

Pupils should be taught to:

a *compose and control their movements by varying shape, size, level, direction, speed and tension.* It has been said that every Dance lesson should include contrast and variety, almost like a good meal. The movement elements providing contrast and variety include: changes of shape and size (e.g. curled in on oneself, clicking fingers, or huge, explosive, star-shaped leap with full arm extension); changes of level or direction (e.g. rising, advancing to high on tip toes, or sinking and turning on the spot); changes of speed and tension (e.g. gently, slowly, gliding and turning, or rushing, reaching, vigorously straight ahead).

Pupils should be able to show that they can:

a *respond imaginatively to the various challenges.* The pupils plan their own actions in one half of the dance and then plan contrasting actions in the other half. In pupil-centred lessons such as this, with pupils free to be original and creative, the teacher must be observant and demonstrate with good examples so that he or she, and the class, see, enjoy and learn from the good ideas.

Lesson Plan – 30 minutes

Theme:
Responding to music to express ideas.

WARM-UP ACTIVITIES - 5 minutes

1 In a previous lesson I told you that the piece of music made me think of flying bubbles, balloons or snowflakes. Today's piece of classical music makes me think of the tiny beginnings of a stream from its slow trickling, hillside start, through its rushing, splashing middle over rocks and waterfalls, to its full width, majestic river climax as it travels on towards the sea.

2 Kneel down and let your gentle hand and arm actions make the early trickling, seeping, creeping action of the drops of hill water as they first appear.

3 Rise up higher on your knees to make these curving, water patterns become bigger. The curving movements can run out forwards, or they can be a side towards impression of the tiny water flow, curving out of the hillside, and starting to trickle downwards.

4 Once again, crouch very low. Show me your two first stages, your 'small beginnings' from seeping, small action start to hillside trickle, as you become taller, making the curving actions bigger.

MOVEMENT SKILLS TRAINING - 12 minutes

1 On your feet now, show me tiny floor patterns, little curves, on a figure 8 as the new stream drops down a little step, and then swirls back on itself.

2 We did 'contrasts' in our last lesson. Can you contrast these slow curling movements, curling round a bend, with the quicker bubbling over stones?

3 Using hands in space, trace the pattern of the water. Everything so far has been in a small space. We can alternate the gentle, slow, trickling, curving in and out and around on its figure 8, with the bubbling and speeding up over the small rocks, using hand patterns in space.

4 Make your curving, travelling floor pattern bigger and feel it with your whole body, not just your feet and arms.

5 Your growing stream meanders, curving, swirling, dropping and bubbling over stones and rocks with a rush and a crash.

6 At the waterfalls, change levels, splashing up, then spreading and diving down.

7 Emphasise the interesting contrasts – dashing over rocks; splashing up and spreading and tumbling down; and the long, slow, smoother curving patterns.

8 Still by yourself, use the whole floor space with your big, slow, sweeping curves that change speed as you go round a boulder, along a fast, narrow bit, or crash over a waterfall.

1 Make groups of three, taking turns to be the leader who can be crouched like a rock for the other two to negotiate, going over or around. They can follow the leader, speeding through narrows, tumbling down and swirling back on themselves, and crashing out in space before tumbling down the waterfalls.

2 The small tributaries of trios gradually come in from the sides or the centre of the room and join the ever-growing, expanding and widening river, as it settles down to a smoother, steadier, almost uninterrupted flow.

3 Let's try the whole dance from the hillside beginnings and source of it all.

Music Smetana's *Ma vlast* (My Fatherland), second movement, by the Boston Symphony Orchestra (3 mins 44 secs).

Time

0 secs All start, well-spaced apart, crouched low to the floor. The water seeps out gently and slowly. The rising and sinking of your chest, only, can express 'Something is coming'.

12 secs Add in gentle arm actions as the river's life starts to appear, with flexible curving patterns by hands only, then arms, then body, low still on the spot.

25 secs Gradually rise up on to your knees and make your curving patterns bigger. Are you showing the water trickling away ahead of you, down the hill, or from a side-on view?

45 secs terns, sometimes in a figure 8, as your stream drops and then turns back on itself. Can you show me both slow, curving movements, round bends in the stream, and faster bubbling as you crash over stones?

1 min 0 secs Show me, with your arm movements in space, how your stream expands from its slow, curving and trickling back on itself to its speeding and bubbling over stones.

1 min 25 secs Use more space as you use your whole body and show the growing line of your expanding stream as it makes its swirling, meandering progress, bubbling up and over stones or dropping to the next level down.

1 min 40 secs Waterfalls, now, and changing levels, as you splash and spread upwards, then dive down to re-join the stream for the next and contrasting, long, slow, curving pattern.

1 min 55 secs By yourself still, use lots of space for your big, slow, sweeping curves that suddenly change speed as you meet a fast, narrow section, or a big boulder, or a sudden waterfall.

2 mins 20 secs In groups of three, take turns at being the leader, sometimes being still for the others to go over or round, and sometimes being the leader, speeding down a narrow section or crashing out in space before you tumble down a waterfall.

2 mins 50 secs Groups of threes come in to join together and make an ever-growing, ever-widening river which settles down, smoothly and steadily into an almost regular, undisturbed flow. (Dance ends at 3 mins 44 secs.)

LESSON NOTES AND NC GUIDANCE

Pupils should be taught to:

a *respond to music.*

b *express ideas.* Pupils will be asked 'Does the music make you imagine anything? What kind of movements can you see?' When 'Stream or river in the countryside' has been agreed, they can be challenged to suggest ideas for the kinds of movement inspired by the changing phrases of the music – small, slow, on the spot; small, gentle, trickling along; bigger, swirling, using more space; faster, crashing, splashing; stronger, bigger, wider; smoothly, steadily, settling to a quieter, straighter flow.

Lesson Plan – 30 minutes

Theme:
Traditional folk dance.

WARM-UP ACTIVITIES - 6 minutes

1 In your lines of four behind a leader, travel to all parts of the room, looking for good spaces. Focus on and copy your leader's travelling actions. Learn and remember these actions.

2 When I call 'Change!' the leader peels off to the end of the line. Number two leader focuses on the upper body, handclaps and gestures to accompany the known actions.

3 Number three leader concentrates on the size of the steps and the effort being used, contrasting, for example, neat, small, quiet skipping with big, strong, lively, skipping.

4 The last leader concentrates on the 'Where?' and occasionally dancing on the spot, alternating with travelling in various directions, not always forwards.

TEACH AND DANCE - Simi Yadech (An Israeli Folk Dance) - 16 minutes

Music *Simi Yadech*, Society for International Folk Dancing.

A lively dance, performed either in a circle or an open circle with a leader at each end. Start clockwise. Hands are held low.

1 Eight Mayim steps clockwise, starting with right foot, travelling sideways to your left.

2 Travel anti-clockwise, forwards, hands by your sides.

Beat	1	Step forwards on right foot.
	2	Hop on right foot.
	3	Step forwards on left foot.
	4	Hop on left foot.
	5	Step forwards on right foot.
	6	Hop on right foot.

3 As **2** (6 step hops in all).

4 With body bending forwards quickly:

step forwards on right foot

step forwards on left foot

step forwards on right foot

step forwards on left foot.

5 Repeat **4**

Mayim Step

Beat	1	Step right foot across in front of left foot.
	2	Step left foot to left.
	3	Step right foot behind left foot.
	4	Step left foot to left.

REVISE A FAVOURITE DANCE OR DANCES - 8 minutes

These can be folk dances such as 'Cumberland Reel', 'Djatchko Kolo', 'Farmer's Jig', 'Wrona Gapa' or 'Three Meet' from previous lessons and years, or, for variety, creative dances learned and remembered.

LESSON NOTES AND NC GUIDANCE

Pupils should be taught to:

a *respond readily to instructions.* In a quick dance with quite difficult steps, it is essential that all look at and listen to the teacher demonstrating and explaining the actions and the figures of the dance.

b *be physically active, engaging in activities that develop the heart and lungs.* Folk dances are the most physically demanding areas of a dance programme. Each lasts for about three minutes of non-stop action, often, as here, with everyone dancing continuously from start to finish. Vigorous action in the big muscles of the legs stimulates and develops the heart and lungs.

c *perform a number of dances from different times and places.* Certain folk dances, such as this, express the particular style and music of the country's national dance.

Pupils should be able to show that they can:

a *repeat and remember a series of movements performed previously.* In a folk dance lesson with a well-behaved, responsive class, there should be time at the end of the lesson for the teacher to ask 'Which of your favourite dances would you like to finish with?' or for the teacher to include a dance that he or she would like to revise, or a more gentle dance to contrast with this lively new one.

Lesson Plan – 30 minutes

Theme:
Feelings.

WARM-UP ACTIVITIES - 5 minutes

1 Skip to this lively folk dance music with its obvious eight-count phrasing. Keep to the rhythm and feel the sets of eight counts. Go! Skip, 2, 3, 4, 5, 6, 7, 8; travel, travel, 3, 4, find spaces, 7, 8; quietly, neatly, 3, 4, skip and skip, 7, 8; silent skipping, 3, 4, 5, 6, 7, stop!

2 Well done. You all kept exactly with the music. Can you now show me a change with each new group of eight counts? It can be a change of direction, size of steps, body shape within your skipping, or a change of action. Travelling and thinking . . . . begin!

MOVEMENT SKILLS TRAINING - 10 minutes

1 Dance lessons, where we express feelings through movement, are difficult. However, you are a brilliant class, so it should be no problem. Show me your proud walking, your proud head and your straight back after being called 'brilliant'.

2 I can see lots of cocky head positions with huge shoulder swaggering. Well done, proud dancers.

3 I am terribly sorry. I made a mistake. You really are a rotten class. Show me your angry stamping, clenching of fists and other movements that express your anger towards me!

4 How dare you stamp your feet at me! You will all be reported and severely punished! Show me a shape that expresses fear. Now travel, showing fear towards something as you creep away, hiding, avoiding, cringing, escaping.

5 Stop creeping away like 'wimps'! Stand up for yourselves! Turn, advance and be aggressive towards the thing or the person. Flex your muscles and get after it. Show who is the boss. Go!

DANCE - Feelings - 15 minutes

1 Well done, my expressive class. Make groups of five, please.

2 You are going to agree on a feeling that your group would like to express in movement. Ideas on this card include happy; sad; frightened; angry; surprised; aggressive; miserable; exhausted; shy; disgusted; shocked; lonely; bored; puzzled; determined.

3 In your planning, you might want to have one of the group as the focus of your sadness, anger, aggression, shock, fear, misery or whatever. Remember, as you focus with your eyes, it is your body movement that is telling me about your inner feelings.

4 Decide on the size of your little stage, how and where will you move from a still starting position and group shape, through your movement, to your still group positon and shape at the end? You will be able to remember your movements more easily if you have a repeating pattern. (For example, cocky head lift; cocky head lift; swagger, swagger, swagger; or angry stamp, stamp, stamp of feet; punch, punch, punch hand against hand.)

5 Have another two complete practices, then you will present your 'Feelings' dance to the other groups who will be challenged to 'Guess what feelings are being expressed through movement. Can you work out what the focus of these feelings are? (e.g. sadness for a dead pet budgie; fear of a monster; aggression towards a bully; disgust towards a litter lout; shocked by an electric current).'

LESSON NOTES AND NC GUIDANCE

Physical Education should involve pupils in:

a *the continuous process of planning, performing and evaluating. The greatest emphasis should be on the actual performance.* In the middle part of the lesson there is a rapid series of challenges to plan and perform a response. 'Show me your proud walking . . . . angry stamping . . . . frightened creeping . . . . aggressive advancing . . . .' There will be several repetitions for improvement, helped by one's own reflecting in response to the teacher's questioning: 'What are the main body movement expressions of pride . . . . anger . . . . fear . . . . aggression?' Reflection guides further planning for an improved performance in this dual physical and education process.

In the group dance climax of the lesson, evaluation will be done by another group who are asked 'Please watch the group and tell me which feelings they are expressing. What movement ideas were particularly clear and expressive? Is there any way they might improve their little dance?'

Pupils should be taught to:

a *express feelings, moods and ideas*

b *respond to a range of stimuli, through Dance.* Varied stimuli contribute greatly to pupils' looking forward to Dance lessons. It is hoped, for example, that a range of stimuli that this year includes actions, opposites, patterns, words on cards, percussion, a film story, winter words, traditional folk dances, contrasts, a river, feelings and voice sounds, will provide something of interest for everyone, and help to give the class a varied and interesting repertoire.

Lesson Plan – 30 minutes

Theme:
Vocal sounds accompaniment and stimulus for movement.

WARM-UP ACTIVITIES - 5 minutes

1 We can accompany dance with recorded music, instruments, body part sounds such as clapping, and voice sounds. Follow me as I travel all round the room and accompany me with your good voice sounds, copying my actions. A helpful rhythm will be appreciated.

2 I liked the 'Toom, toom, toom, toom' with my marching; the 'Tick, tock, tick, tock' with my slow, feet astride, stepping; the loud humming as I turned; and the 'Boomp, boomp, boomp, boomp' with my bouncing.

MOVEMENT SKILLS TRAINING - 10 minutes

1 Find a partner and decide who is the mover and who is the voice accompaniment. Mover, can you vary your actions, staying on the spot, only? Do small, smooth movements for a small, smooth, continuous sound from your partner.

2 Now try a bigger action which might be a stop/start to invite a louder, jerky, on/off sound.

3 Rise and fall, mover, to give your partner an interesting variety of sounds to make. Changing speed would be good to see and hear.

4 Change places, please. The new mover will travel, not too far or fast, with the sound-making partner travelling and making some brilliant, unique sounds.

5 Travelling partner, please vary your actions to include, for example, slow, smooth, jerky, big, small to give your sound-making partner plenty of variety, making sounds never heard before.

6 Let's have each half of the class performing and sound making for the other half. Watch and listen for brilliant partnerships to tell me about, so that we can share really good ideas.

DANCE - Voice Sounds - 15 minutes

1 Form groups of five. Sit down and discuss a favourite idea for a holidays 'Voice Sounds' dance. You may elongate or shorten action words, (Pl-a-a-a-ay te-e-n-n-is); place names, (The R—i-v i-i—era); favourite food, (Ba-a-a-a-nan-a split); or invent sounds or words to accompany your holiday actions.

2 Are you thinking of an enjoyable holiday sporting action; a favourite holiday resort; or food, glorious food? Decide, then start to work out your accompanying actions as a group.

3 Sporting action will be represented by the actions, ultra slow, normal speed or speeded up, if you can shorten the word.

4 Place names and food can be accompanied by an interesting mixture of travelling, jumping, turning, rising, falling, gesturing and stillness – long, drawn out, normal speed or accelerated to make it eye-catching and funny.

5 Agree your starting shapes and finishing shapes as a group.

6 Try to include actions that make a short, repeating pattern to help you to remember them easily. Keep practising.

7 For your demonstrations, one group at a time, try to be expressing 'Our choice of sport, or resort, or food, is the best – just like our movement. Watch how well we work together. Watch our larger than life movements and listen to our super sounds.'

LESSON NOTES AND NC GUIDANCE

Pupils should be able to show that they can:

a *respond imaginatively to the various challenges.* Both partners are being challenged to make imaginative and very different responses. 'Mover, can you . . . . ? Sound accompanist, can you make a matching sound?' Groups are challenged to plan an imaginative, holiday idea, and then perform it with an accompanying sound.

b *practise, improve and refine performance.* This last lesson of the year gives great freedom to the pupils in the decision-making and organisation of their practising. It is hoped that the created actions and sounds will be surprising, humorous, varied, a tribute to their enthusiasm, energy, and 'togetherness' as a class, and an enjoyable climax to the year's programme.

c *make simple judgements about others' performances to improve the accuracy, quality and variety of the performance.* From year three onwards, observers should have been trained to value demonstrations; be appreciative and sensitive observers; express pleasure and encouragement when evaluating others' achievements; and make helpful, friendly comments regarding areas that might be improved.

Lesson Plan – 30 minutes

Theme:
Rhythmic patterns.

1 Show me your best stepping in time with this medium-speed music. If I beat my drum loudly on count eight each time, can you introduce a change – style or size of step, body shape, firmness of whole body, or direction, for example? Best stepping, go! Best stepping, spacing well, 5, 6, 7 and change! Keep practising.

2 Well done. I saw changes to step size; stepping with high knees; stepping and closing sideways (as in folk dance chasse); sliding steps; stepping with feet apart; and very relaxed and very firm stepping.

3 Leaping is like high, wide running or stepping. Do four lively leaps, then four 'easy' actions on the spot. Go! Leap and leap and leap for 4; on the spot, 3, 4; leap high, leap long, for 3, for 4; easy action, 3, 4; leap and leap and leap for 4; keep going.

4 I liked your contrasting big/lively and small/easy movements.

1 Still working in groups of eight counts, can you stay on the spot and show me a pattern of favourite actions or movements? May I suggest stepping, bouncing, skipping, clapping, gesturing or turning? Two or more actions, neatly linked, and contrasting, will be excellent. Go! On the spot, on the spot, 5, 6, 7 and change; new action, contrast action, 5, 6, 7, again!

2 Well done. That looked really good and I enjoyed the many shapes as you put your whole body into it.

3 Now for favourite travelling actions. We have used steps and leaps of all sorts. You might want to add skipping, bouncing, running and galloping. Can you show me your varied travelling pattern, with eight counts to each one? Go! Travel, 2, 3, 4, 5, 6, 7, change; new travel, 3, 4, 5, 6, change again!

DANCE - Patterns on a Stage - 12 minutes

1 The middle third of the hall is going to be your stage for the final part of our lesson. It extends from side to side, from this line to that line and is quite big.

2 Start off the stage, walk to the edge of the stage and then do a two-part travelling action pattern to take you on to the stage. On the spot, you will then do your two-part pattern. After that, you will make your way off-stage to the other end with the same, or a different, two-part travelling action pattern.

3 While you are waiting off-stage, look for a good space before you come on-stage again to repeat your three patterns – the travelling on-stage; the on the spot; and the travelling from the stage.

4 I will stand at the side of your stage to watch your on-stage performance. Pretend I am a talent scout and do your very best.

5 Each half of the class will now watch the other half from the side of the stage. Spectators, you may quietly clap any impressive performance as the dancer leaves the stage, and be able to tell us what you particularly liked about him or her.

6 Spectators, look for neat movements using the whole body in larger than life activity; good, clear, proud body shapes; and varied use of directions and body tension, both firm and gentle.

LESSON NOTES AND NC GUIDANCE

Pupils should be taught to:

a *recognise the safety risks of wearing inappropriate jewellery, footwear and clothing.*

b *respond readily to instructions.*

c *be mindful of others.*

d *adopt the best possible posture and use of the body.*

e *be physically active.* This checklist of essential features should be established, if necessary, with a class at the start of a new school year. The highest possible standards of safety, progress and achievement will never be achieved if a class:

* is badly-dressed, wearing jewellery; long leg coverings that catch heels; large, heavy, noisy ungiving 'trainers'; or unbunched long hair that impedes vision.

* behaves badly by incessantly talking; failing to listen and respond to instructions – particularly to 'Stop!'

* contains anti-social elements who rush around at high speed, disturbing others, selfishly ignoring the need of others for a reasonable space to work in; and who do not work co-operatively in partner or group work.

* slouch lazily through the lessons, standing, sitting or moving with sagging posture; never trying wholeheartedly to show a strong, firm, clear shape; never trying to look good.

* continually works at far less than maximum effort; never takes muscle and joint actions to their fullest use; and never gives the impression of breathing deeply and perspiring profusely.

Lesson Plan – 30 minutes

Theme:
Voice sound accompaniment.

WARM-UP ACTIVITIES - 5 minutes

1 No music today! Let's share the voice sound accompaniment in our warm-ups. Feet astride, slowly str-e-e-t-ch every part of your body. You say the next action and decide whether it will be v-e-r-y s-l-o-w or sudden. Go!

2 Once again, my slow str-e-e-t-ch. Now your say. Go!

3 With me, st-e-e-p-p-ing plus st-re-e-t-ching, ultra slow motion with a long stretch in arms, legs and body. Now your travel with a body action – slow motion, normal speed or fast forwards. Go!

4 Let's combine the two pairs of actions with our voices making the accompaniment and the rhythm, on the spot, then moving.

MOVEMENT SKILLS TRAINING - 15 minutes

1 We accompanied ourselves, doing big movements on the spot and travelling, at normal speed, fast and slow. Remember when composing a dance to include the following.

a Jumping. Try on the spot; after a run; from one foot to both; from one to other; two to two; and with wide, long or twisted shapes.

b Turning. Do one on the spot, then one around an enclosed space. Turns are usually long, slow, graceful movements and different parts can lead you – elbow, back, side, shoulder, back of one hand.

c Rising and falling. From a low, still, crouched or lying start, you rise up to start or continue the dance. From upright, can you lower or fall to finish at floor level?

d Open and close. Contrast the opening action of sowing and scattering seeds with the closing action, pulling in a fisherman's nets, in a harvest or sea dance.

e Gesture. Show movements by body parts not supporting weight. A gesture can be expressive: goal!; despair with shoulders sagging; anger with a stamp; surprise with hands suddenly lifted.

f Stillness. Before start; often at the end; sometimes within the dance. Body shape varies, depending on the nature of the movement preceding or following. Be still! Travel . . . . and be still!

1 Use some of the activities we have just practised as you move to different parts of 'Spaghetti Bolognese', making some parts sl-o-o-w and lo-o-o-ng, and some parts quick and maybe explosive. Have a practice, saying the words clearly.

2 Remember to use some of the activities we practised earlier. Can you include, at least, a travel, a jump and stillness?

3 Well done. Now add in a turn, rise and fall, or open and close.

4 Pretend you own an Italian restaurant and are trying to attract lots of customers. Make your dance very expressive and eye catching as you dance and talk your way through it. Go!

5 Very well done. I particularly liked Gary's final gesture with one arm forwards, as if holding a tray for us to admire, almost saying 'I'm the best!'

6 Let's have half of the class looking at and listening to the other half to share all these brilliant ideas.

LESSON NOTES AND NC GUIDANCE

Pupils should be taught to:

a *respond readily to instructions.* The warm-up and the middle part of the lesson contain much direct teaching, with the class being told about ten things to do in reasonably quick succession. An immediate, wholehearted and thoughtful response is essential.

   The planning and performing of the dance climax also requires pupils to listen carefully to the precise details of the challenge, so they can be imaginative and creative during the pupil-centred section of the lesson.

b *be physically active.* It might be appropriate for the teacher to tell the class 'Year Six is the very best age for Physical Education. You are strong and supple, and able to learn physical skills quicker and better than at any subsequent stage. Once a skill is learned by your body it is remembered for a very long time. Please use this school year to work hard in all our lessons and learn as many enjoyable, healthy, sociable and worthwhile physical skills as possible.'

Pupils should be able to show that they can:

a *respond imaginatively to the various challenges.* Year Six pupils can be tremendously imaginative, and another reason for insisting on immediate 'responses to instructions', is the need to make time for demonstrations. Knowing that they will be asked to demonstrate inspires pupils to greater effort, and the demonstrations increase the repertoire of teacher and class.

Lesson Plan – 30 minutes

Theme:
Autumn.

WARM-UP ACTIVITIES - 5 minutes

1 Jim, on top of the high box, is going to throw the leaves I brought in, as high as he can. Watch how they fly in many different ways – particularly with the windows open, to help their flight. Pretend they have just left their branches.

2 Can you try to show me some of the movement qualities seen during their flight? Off you go, flying, gliding, tilting, turning, hovering in unpredictable pathways and directions.

3 Your movements are free, light, sometimes being carried a long way, then held almost on the spot before soaring down and rising quickly.

4 You should all have a different shape like my leaves. Are you flat, crinkly, curled, long, wide, twisted or jagged? Show me.

5 One last flight, please. Think about your shape, light travelling actions, speed changes, and all the spaces you visit. Go!

MOVEMENT SKILLS TRAINING - 12 minutes

1 I enjoyed your wildly unpredictable leaf-like movements. Show me how you might express the movements of a branch on a tree. Can you start in a shape to represent your choice of branch – long, thin and 'bendy'; solid, heavy, unbending; or medium size with lots of lesser, intertwining, branches sprouting in all directions?

2 Show me the distances you think your kind of branch might move in space.

3 Are your movements fast, slow, strong, gentle, or a mixture that depend on the force of the wind and your size and weight?

4 Are some of you able to intertwine with one or both arms with a nearby branch?

1 Show me how you might express the restricted, strong movement of the tree trunk at the heart of our tree. Grip the floor firmly with your feet (roots) and move slowly and firmly.

2 Your speed will be far slower than the branches or leaves and will involve your whole body as it sways in all directions.

3 Practise again your branch-like movements which depend on your size and shape. Feel the greater freedom and greater distances travelled after the very restricted trunk. Intertwine with a similar branch next to you, if you like.

4 Change to practising movements that express the very free, light, variable speeds of leaves in flight.

5 For our 'Autumn Trees' dance, there will be three groups: the trunk group at the centre; the branches group as an inner circle; and the outside leaves group, attached at first, then breaking free and flying away. Practise your actions and see if they can be fitted into a repeating pattern. Can you include a voice accompaniment as we did in the previous lesson? Creaking trunks, groaning branches, swooshing leaves?

6 Be ready to start, everyone. Build up from a soft, gentle wind, to medium strength, to a raging gale with increasing volume sound accompaniment. Good movement and good sound, please. Begin!

LESSON NOTES AND NC GUIDANCE

Physical Education should involve pupils in:

a *the continuous process of planning, performing and evaluating. The greatest emphasis should be placed on the actual performance.* It is fair and sensible to put the class 'in the picture' regarding the aims of each new lesson, particularly if there is to be some assessment of their achievement. They should be told the nature of the hoped-for achievement.

'In National Curriculum Physical Education, the three most important headings are "planning, performing and evaluating". In all your lessons I want to feel that you are planning, thinking ahead, and making your own good decisions about what actions to do, where to do them, and how to do them.

'We are lucky in Physical Education because it is easy to see the whole class performing from all parts of the room. I want to see you working hard to do a neat, quiet, well-controlled, poised performance – and be able to remember and repeat it for me.

"Evaluating" means that you watch others performing, or think about your own work, and then make helpful comments about what you liked, about the important features and quality of the movements, and maybe suggest ways in which the performance can be improved.

'In our "Autumn Leaves" dance, you will be asked to plan and show me the three very different kinds of movement typical of the tree trunk, its branches and its leaves. I will look forward to seeing (and listening!) to your stylish performances. Then, each of the three groups in turn will perform and be watched by the other two who will reflect on what impressed them. The helpful comments and suggestions will then be used to improve our next practice.'

Lesson Plan – 30 minutes

Theme Contrasts in body tension.

Music Eastenders theme.

WARM-UP ACTIVITIES - 5 minutes

1 This slow, Eastenders music, with its eight-count phrasing, is perfect for slow travelling steps and big movements. Step slowly to the music. Slow, slow, 3, 4, 5, 6, keep on going.

2 Add a full body bend and stretch as you travel. You can stretch on the odd numbers, bend on the evens. Go! Stretch and bend for 3 and 4, stretch and bend for 7, repeat.

3 For variety, can you reach out, up or down for your stretches and bendings, always accompanied by your slow, rhythmic stepping?

MOVEMENT SKILLS TRAINING - 12 minutes

Phrase 1 Stretching out strongly and curling back gently.

1 Sit down near a partner, without touching, in a position from which you can move your whole body into a full, firm stretch.

2 Which part of your body will lead into your stretch? (An arm, leg or one of each, probably.) Ready? Stretch firmly, 3 and 4. Hold your whole body stretch with no sagging parts.

3 Curl in gently and take four counts to arrive. Let the curl come right in towards your middle. Ready? Curl in, 3 and 4.

Phrase 2 Stretch strongly, curl back gently, but with a different part or parts stretching out into a different shape. The easy, gentle curl back ends in a kneeling position, all facing front.
Stretch firmly, 3, 4; curl back gently, kneel to face the front.

Phrase 3 Right hand stretch up, left hand stretch up, curl back to starting position (four counts up, four counts down). Kneel tall, facing front and stretch strongly upwards, 1 and 2, with your right hand. Left hand follows, 3 and 4. Both arms gently curl down together, returning to position as at start of dance, four counts.

Phrases 4 and 5 Repeat **phrases 1 and 2**.

Phrase 6 Walk to meet your partner, ready for shared stretches. All travel for six counts, meet partner and go down into the very first position during counts seven and eight.

Phrases 7 and 8 Stretch out firmly and contact partner with a body part. Curl in gently. Stretch out strongly again, making contact again. Curl in and hold your final position still.

DANCE - Stretching and Curling - 8 minutes

1 Sit near your partner. Stretch up and curl down, eight counts.

2 Stretch up and curl down, with a different body part stretching up.

3 Kneel, all facing the front, right hand stretch up, left hand stretch up, both hands curl back down.

4 Stretch up and bend down; stretch up and bend down.

5 Walk to meet your partner. From dance start position, stretch with body contact twice with your partner. Finish, curled still.

LESSON NOTES AND NC GUIDANCE

Pupils should be taught to:

a *respond to music.*

b *respond to a range of stimuli, through Dance.* Music is one of the many varied stimuli used to make lessons interesting. In Year Six these include: actions, patterns, voice sounds, nature, percussion, country dance steps and figures, follow the leader, a bible story and work actions.

The slow, Eastenders music inspires whole body, slow movements that contrast with the much quicker music of other lessons

c *compose and control their movements by varying shape, size, level and tension.* With the short phrasing of the music it is easy to repeat, practise and refine the firm, strong, whole body stretches with different parts to different levels, and to contrast them with the more gentle curling back in to oneself.

Pupils should be able to show that they can:

a *repeat sequences with increasing control and accuracy.* This is a short dance with few, simple movements. The movements are performed slowly, allowing lots of time to do each one carefully and thoughtfully. Demonstrations, with couples observing other couples, lead to a sharing of good ideas. The teacher's accompanying rhythm serves both as a reminder of what is happening, and an encouragement to greater quality. 'Stretch out strongly, whole body firm; curl back gently, easily for four.'

Lesson Plan – 30 minutes

Theme:
Christmas and sharing.

WARM-UP ACTIVITIES - 5 minutes

1 Stand facing a partner, about two metres apart. One starts as leader, the other watches and mirrors the actions and movements shown. The music is medium/slow to help you keep together. Start off, leader, with an action on the spot, using your legs. Go!

2 Can you make your action travel, for example to one side, then back; or to leader's rear, then forwards? Mirroring partner goes the opposite way, of course.

3 Once again, perform on the spot, then travel, then on the spot, then travel, making a repeating pattern.

4 Do it all again with the following partner adding a simple, accompanying body movement for the original leader to copy. It can be a simple clapping on the spot and a gesturing of arms on the move – or something more adventurous if you like.

5 We might call this 'A double follow the leader' or 'Two mirrors on a moving wall.' Well done. Keep practising.

MOVEMENT SKILLS TRAINING - 15 minutes

1 Start in a big circle where you can all see me. Listen to the rhythmic, medium/slow tempo of the music and all say with me 'Watch it, pass it on' keeping with the beat of the music.

2 Watch my simple action as you say 'Watch it' and then copy it as you say 'Pass it on.'

3 Watch it again on the 'Watch it', but on the 'Pass it on' turn to the person on your right and present the action in their direction. This gives practice in the passing on, even if that person is busy doing the same thing to his or her right.

4 Watch me carefully as I do a four-part routine, with each action being shown once only. 'Watch it (e.g. a handclap), Pass it on, Watch it (e.g. a small step forwards and back with one foot), Pass it on, Watch it (e.g. knees bend and stretch), Pass it on, Watch it (e.g. jump to wide position, arms stretched), Pass it on.' Very well done. Most of you kept with me and passed it on.

5 Will anyone volunteer to think of four actions to lead the class through, please? Thank you, Laura. We are all ready for our next 'Watch it, Pass it on.' Begin when you are ready, please.

6 Thank you, Laura, and well done. Can we have a boy volunteer now, please? Thank you, Brian. Start when ready, please.

DANCE - Pass the Movement Parcel - 10 minutes

1 Make circles of five. Your leader will do a four-action repeating sequence, calling out 'Watch it, Pass it on.' Begin.

2 That was easy. Now, with a new leader, try the more difficult passing on, only to the next person. Number two watches the leader and passes it on to number three who watches it and passes it on to number four who passes it on to number five. After two has passed it on, he or she looks back at the leader to see the new action, then passes it on to number three who watches it and passes it on to number four, and so on. Eventually the 'passed on' actions come back to the leader who continues to pass them on.

3 Let's have a look at each 'Passing on' circle in turn.

LESSON NOTES AND NC GUIDANCE

Pupils should be taught to:

a *respond readily to instructions.* This lesson, with its three stages of development – mirroring another; 'watching another and passing it on'; and a group 'watching and passing it on' – is quite difficult and requires concentration and attention, by everyone, for an enjoyable and successful outcome.

b *be mindful of others.* 'Others' include a partner to whom you are showing good quality movements of which your partner is capable; the partner whose actions you are mirroring to the best of your ability for joint success; the teacher in the middle of the lesson on whom you are concentrating totally; and your team-mates in the dance climax for whom you are trying your hardest, before the inevitable demonstration by your group.

c *respond to a range of stimuli, through Dance.* Lesson by lesson, increasingly varied stimuli make Dance lessons more interesting, exciting and enjoyable. Eventually the varied challenges make the dancers more skilful and versatile. The topical, Christmas 'Pass the Movement Parcel' dance is completely different to anything they have done before.

Pupils should be able to show that they can:

a *practise, improve and refine performance.* A suggested approach to practising and improving performance is to have a three-stage development plan:

1 clarify the actions, the body parts concerned and the clear shapes.

2 add interest by varying directions, levels and good use of the space all around.

3 clarify the amount of effort or speed that is just right.

Lesson Plan – 30 minutes

Theme:
Winter.

WARM-UP ACTIVITIES - 5 minutes

1 With a partner, do 'Follow the leader' where the leader shows lively, travelling actions that use every joint to warm you up. Keep in time with the medium-speed music. Go!

2 Stop! The other partner will now lead in whole body, lively actions on the spot. Once again, try to use every joint and muscle in your body. Try to mirror your leader exactly. Begin!

3 In your two-part, winter warm-up, travel to a good space, then face each other for your on the spot actions. Keep with the phrasing of the music as you do your repeating patterns. Go!

MOVEMENT SKILLS TRAINING - 15 minutes

1 Your deeper breathing and perspiring faces tell me that you warmed up successfully. Well done. One of your couple will now collect a piece of percussion while the other collects one of my three different sets of cards with their three winter words.

Set 1 Birds in winter wind
FLUTTER   SOAR   SWIRL

Set 2 Snow
DRIFT   FREEZE   MELT

Set 3 People
STAMP   SLIP   SHIVER

2 Put your card down on the floor. Study the words and plan how your movements will clearly represent the words.

3 Number one dancer, practise your three actions clearly for your partner to watch. Start when ready, without any percussion.

4 Dancer, your partner will give you one helpful comment to improve your performance. Were the actions correct? Did they express clearly the main movement qualities of the actions? Were the shapes clear? Was the timing too hurried or too slow?

5 Same dancer again, please, accompanied by partner on percussion. Percussionist, quietly accompany your partner, starting and stopping each time to make the three actions separate.

6 Well done. The improvements were obvious. Now change places.

7 New dancers, stand ready, please. No accompaniment yet as partner watches to see what might be improved. Begin when ready.

8 Dancers, your partner will tell you one thing that might be improved. Can the main movement feature be expressed better? Can the whole body be more involved? What about an exciting contrast in effort or speed?

9 Same dancers with percussion this time. Each action is started and stopped by the percussion. Start when ready, please.

10 Well done, dancers and partners whose advice produced an obvious improvement.

1 I have placed your couple next to a couple with a different set of winter words. Hide your card so they can't read the words.

2 Each couple in turn will perform twice, working as dancer and percussionist to see if the other couple recognise your words.

3 Do it all again. Observers, please watch and then tell the other couple what you particularly liked in their demonstrations.

LESSON NOTES AND NC GUIDANCE

Pupils should be taught to:

a *adopt the best possible posture and use of the body.* We want the dancers to be conscious of their whole body in expressing the different qualities of their three action words. Before they start, they should be asked 'Show me by your starting posture what your first action is.' Arms, shoulders, head and spine, as well as legs, all need to be used to express the lightweight, hovering, 'flutter'; the gentle, travelling 'drift'; or the firm, heavy 'stamp'.

b *respond readily to instructions.* The short sequences will only be improved by listening carefully and responding to the helpful, general teaching points and individual coaching by the teacher, and by trying to respond to the one main suggestion for improvement made by the partner.

c *respond to a range of stimuli, through Dance.* The three-fold stimuli include seasonal action words, percussion, and an observing partner/coach, in addition to the ever-present stimulus of an enthusiastic, appreciative teacher.

Pupils should be able to show that they can:

a *make simple judgements about another's performance to improve the accuracy, quality and variety of the performance.* The observing percussion partner can be asked 'Please put up your hand if you think your dancer improved as a result of your advice. You will then be asked to identify the improvement.'

Lesson Plan – 30 minutes

Theme:
Creative, traditional folk dance.

WARM-UP ACTIVITIES - 5 minutes

1 Take eight steps of the music to travel from space to space. Use any steps, including some you make up. Arrive in your new space on eight and dance on the spot for eight, using steps we have learned or your own creation. Travelling, and on the spot, in counts of eight, go!

2 Stop! Join with a partner, dance together to your next space, then do eight steps on the spot. One leads with the follower remembering the steps. Follower leads on the spot with partner remembering.

3 Each of you decided a part of the dance, watched by the other. Can you now keep going, copying actions as you travel, and then as you stay – always using eight counts of the music for each?

NEW FIGURES FOR GROUPS OF FOUR - 15 minutes

1 Make a square of four dancers anywhere in the room. This is not a set with first and second couples. It is simply a group of four who will not travel outside their own floor space area as you try some new ideas for folk dance figures, taking eight counts.

a 1 2 1 dances to 2's position with two travelling steps.
2 dances to 4's position. 4 dances to

3 4 3's position.
3 dances to 1's position.
Repeat in the other direction for 8 more counts, 1 starting.

b 1 2 1 and 4 dance to change places for 2 counts.
2 and 3 dance to change places.

3 4 1 and 4 return to own places.
2 and 3 return to own places.

c 1 2 1 and 4 make an arch with hands joined for 2 and 3 to dance under to change places for 4 counts. Arch

3 4 remains for 2 and 3 to dance back to places for 4 counts. Repeat with 2 and 3 making an arch for 1 and 4.

d 1 2 3 and 2 join hands for a tiny circle left and right.
1 and 4 dance in a bigger circle, 4

3 4 counts to the right and 4 back to left to own places.

e 1 2 1 leads 2 across, outside the line of 3 and 4 and back round square to own side and starting places for 8 counts.

3 4 Repeat with 3 leading 4 across and round the square for 8 counts.

f Can you think of any other interesting figure that does not take you away from your own group floor space?

Four figures will be linked together and it is good to have everyone dancing for the last 8 counts. This might be the one you create as your climax. For example, all step forwards, joining and raising hands to a peak, then stepping out backwards. Good ideas will be demonstrated, shared, praised and sometimes copied.

LESSON NOTES AND NC GUIDANCE

Pupils should be involved in:

a *the continuous process of planning, performing and evaluating, and the greatest emphasis should be on the actual performance.* Planning and creativity can both be indulged in a folk dance setting. The class repertoire will ideally include '2002 folk dances' in addition to those from 'different times and places'.

Programme of Study. Pupils should be taught to:

a *respond to music.* The eight-bar phrasing in the warm-up; the eight-count figures of the middle of the lesson; and the four by eight bar extent of the created dance, all make the class aware of the beat of the music to be followed. Teacher chanting helps to keep the dancers in time with the music, and is a reminder of what is happening. 'Your first figure, 3, 4, 5, 6, ready to change; second figure, 3, 4, 5, 6, third figure, now . . . .'

b *perform a number of dances, including some traditional dances of the British Isles.* The music here is traditional as is the travelling step and the slipping step sideways in the circle. The figures are traditional as they change places, make arches to go under, circle to the left and right, or cast off to their own side. The four figure repeating pattern of the dance is traditional. It is hoped that the excellent posture, the dancing in time with the music, and the sociable togetherness and excellent teamwork typical of good folk dance, are also in evidence.

Pupils should be able to show that they can:

a work safely, sensibly, co-operatively and unselfishly as members of a team. Such an attainment will be expressed in a poised team performance that flows smoothly from start to finish.

b repeat sequences with increasing control and accuracy. The music provides the rhythm and practice will enable the group to remember and repeat their four actions.

Lesson Plan – 30 minutes

Theme:
Traditional folk dance.

WARM-UP ACTIVITIES - 5 minutes

1 Practise skip change of step with a partner who can be beside you, leading, following, or going away from and coming back to you. Let each action have eight counts of the music as a guide.

2 Show me neat foot movements as you hop at the start, then into your travel, 2, 3; lift, travel, 2, 3; lift, step, close up, step.

3 Can you decide which three or four ways you are going to relate to each other? Try to add interesting variety – together; apart; parting and meeting; one still, one going round.

TEACH FIGURES OF NEW DANCE - Dashing White Sergeant - 15 minutes

This is one of the most popular of all Scottish country dances, practised in sixes with three dancers facing three dancers. A boy between two girls faces a girl between two boys. Groups of sixes start in a circle formation around the room.

```
                    O X
                    X O
                    O X
        O X O               X O X
        X O X               O X O
                    X O
                    O X
                    X O
```

1 All six dancers join hands in a circle and dance eight slip steps to the left and eight back to the right.

2 Centre dancer, turn to right hand partner. Set to each other and turn with both hands with four setting steps. Centre dancer, now do this with left hand partner and finish facing to your right.

3 Dance a reel of three (figure of 8), centre dancer starting the reel by giving right shoulder to right hand partner. Eight skip changes of step to finish facing three dancers opposite.

4 All advance and retire, then pass on to meet the three dancers coming towards you, passing right shoulders with the person opposite.

DANCE - Dashing White Sergeant - 10 minutes

Music   *Dashing White Sergeant* or any lively 32-bar tune.

Formation   A circle round the room in threes, one line of three facing clockwise and the other line of three facing anti-clockwise.

Bars 1–8   Circle left and right, eight slipping steps each way.

Bars 9–16   Centre dancer sets to and turns each of their partners.

Bars 17–24   Reel of three, to finish facing opposite trio.

Bars 25–32   Advance and retire and pass on to meet next three dancers and repeat the dance.

LESSON NOTES AND NC GUIDANCE

Pupils should be taught to:

a *be physically active, engaging in activities that develop the heart and lungs.* As well as being one of the most popular of all Scottish country dances, this is one of the most physical. The mixture of travelling, setting and slipping steps, all done at a lively speed, make it one of the most physically demanding. It is guaranteed to inspire deep breathing, lots of perspiration and much enjoyment.

b *be mindful of others.* The team element is high, with all six dancers needing to work and think hard to be in the right place at the right time, and to help one another by careful 'handling' as they place one another in the right positions.

c *perform a number of dances from different times and places, including some traditional dances of the British Isles.* This is a dance that expresses all that is good about lively folk dance. It is fun, friendly, physical; it depends on good team work; performed well, it has flowing, beautiful, attractive movement; and it has a long 'shelf life', able to be repeated and repeated.

Pupils should be able to show that they can:

a *repeat sequences with increasing control and accuracy.* The music provides the guiding, lively rhythm; good teamwork with all pupils thinking ahead ensures the smooth repetition of the four-part pattern of the dance; and good teaching of one main point for each practice ensures an increase in quality.

Lesson Plan – 30 minutes

Theme:
Creating a story with simple characters.

WARM-UP ACTIVITIES - 5 minutes

1 Listen to this anxious, 'rushing around' music, then show me how you might respond to its urgent, somewhat jerky rhythm.

2 Well done. Lots of hither and thither, anxious-looking, hurrying.

3 Can your anxiety include some watch watching to show that you might be late for something as you rush to your meeting place?

4 Be brilliant and produce a repeating pattern of anxious travelling to your destination. This is helped by pretending you are near home with streets, corners and crossings you know.

MOVEMENT SKILLS TRAINING - 15 minutes

1 Our movements represent a group of office workers. At the start our anxious travelling takes us to our bus stop, and we are a little late. All stand ready, at home, in an anxious shape.

2 We have decided the places you are travelling to, for your bus stop queues. Fifteen seconds of worried walking . . . . go!

3 Stand in line at your bus stop. Lean forwards, looking right for the bus and looking at your watch. (Class in lines of four at the several bus stops, spaced around the room.)

Pattern Look for the bus; look at your watch; stamp your feet, temper, temper! (Thrice.)

4 All step straight on to the bus, shoulder to shoulder, squashed, strap hanging with right hand, holding paper with left hand.

Pattern Hang on your strap, hang on your strap; read your paper, read your paper; all stumble to the right. (One at the right hand end stands firm.) Hang on your strap, hang on your strap; read the paper, read the paper; all stumble to the left. (Person at the left hand end stands firm.) Three times, to right, to left, to right.

5 Off the bus and it is a short walk to the office where you all are half sitting at your desk, all in regimental lines, facing towards the same end.

Pattern Pick up your phone; pick up your pen; listen to message; write it down, write it down. Phone down; pen down; type it up, type it up. File it high, file it high (into high drawer). Repeat.

6 Going home. Heavy feet. Tired city workers after a long day.

Five-part dance

Time

0 secs	To bus stop.
15 secs	In bus queue.
32 secs	On to bus.

50 secs	To office desk.
1min 18 secs	Home.
1min 30 secs	Dance ends.

LESSON NOTES AND NC GUIDANCE

Pupils should be taught to:

a *try hard to consolidate performances.* Because the whole dance lasts only one and a half minutes, there are ample opportunities for improving, remembering, and being able to repeat the dance. It is recommended that during each practice or part of the dance, one teaching point only is emphasised. Right at the start the 'What?', or actions, should be clarified, with the body parts concerned and the shapes receiving a special focus. 'Where?', the next focus, considers the locations, possible changes of level or direction and ways to use one's own surrounding air space. 'How?', and interesting use of speed and effort, make a big contribution to the quality and variety of the performance.

b *express feelings, moods and ideas.*

c *create simple characters and stories.* The expression of the moods and feelings of the participants, and the creation of the characters and their story, are both done through movement. Imagery is used throughout to provide interest, understanding of what the dance is all about, and to conjure up easily visualised pictures. We move 'Like early morning commuters, with their anxious, rushing steps.' Our whole body moves 'Like an angry, stamping, bus queue person.'

Imagery is used to help us visualise ourselves clearly in a real situation, and is better than the vague 'We are going to explore feelings. Can you show me "Anger"? Imagery deserves to be included within the 'range of stimuli' that we are required to use in our teaching.

Lesson Plan – 30 minutes

Theme:
Expressing feelings and creating a story.

WARM-UP ACTIVITIES - 5 minutes

1 Practise a punch, without any contact of course, and the reaction to it by your partner. Each of you take turns at being the attacker, and the victim, reacting and staggering backwards.

2 Keep a safe distance apart and show me examples of punches to different parts of the body and the different reactions to them.

3 A punch towards the head has a violent, upper body, staggering reaction backwards. Be very careful. Try it – keeping well apart.

4 Good, punchers and reactors. Now, well apart, try a long distance kick towards your partner's abdomen. This should produce a crumpling, folding, extremely painful reaction.

5 Attacker, grab your partner by the shoulders or arms. Try a quick twist and a very careful lowering of your partner, right down safely to the floor.

6 Well done, all couples. That was very sensibly practised and I saw many realistic actions and the expected reactions.

MOVEMENT SKILLS TRAINING - 10 minutes

1 Join with another couple now and decide who is to be the victim, the puncher, the kicker, and the grabber and twister.

2 Victim, work in the field at your own choice of action – raking, digging or sowing. Attackers, spread out to surround the victim, ready for the attack.

3 Puncher, you come in from the front of the victim and your punch repels the victim backwards, turning him or her towards the kicker. The kick to the lower tummy crumples him or her. The third attacker reaches down and in, gripping on shoulders or arms, to twist and lower the victim all the way to the ground.

4 Please practise with great care, keeping a very safe distance apart on the punch and kick, and remembering to twist and lower the victim all the way to the floor. No judo throws! Lower gently.

5 May I see each group in turn to check on your safe actions and reactions. Very carefully, first group, begin.

'A certain man went down from Jerusalem to Jericho, and fell among thieves. They wounded him and departed, leaving him half dead. A priest saw him but passed by on the other side. A Levite came and looked at him and passed by on the other side. But a certain Samaritan saw him, had compassion and bound up his wounds. He set him on his own beast and took care of him.'

1 With your body movements, aim to express the feelings and emotions of the four groups in our dance.

2 Starting positions, please, with the victim working in the field.

3 Perform the fight sequence as we practised. Thieves, get into your attacking positions, surrounding the victim. Advance slowly and menacingly to punch, then kick, then grab and lower.

4 Victim lies wounded by the roadside. Thieves, walk away, moving towards the next victim, to represent another group on the busy road. You approach and look away as you come near this next victim. You 'pass by on the other side' pretending 'it's none of our business.'

5 Trios, move towards the next victim. This group expresses some concern. One bends to touch the victim, but all then 'pass by on the other side' again.

6 Trios, progress on to the next victim and your attitude shows a change for the better as you all try to help, in a disorganised way. One of you becomes leader and good Samaritan and organises the other two to lift the wounded victim very gently and slowly to his or her feet.

7 Victim, you are now strongly supported by the three encircling you, pushing you towards each other as their hands encourage life, movement and recovery.

8 In harmony, you all walk along together as friends, expressing compassion and caring.

9 Well done, everyone. You provided an interesting variety of expressions – the terrified victim; the cruel trio with their violence; the unconcerned; the semi-concerned, half-hearted, dithering third group; and the caring last group, led by the good Samaritan.

LESSON NOTES AND NC GUIDANCE

Pupils should be taught to:

a *express feelings, moods and ideas.*

b *create simple ideas and stories.* Feelings of aggression, menace, cruelty, pain, fear, disinterest, compassion and caring, as well as the story idea, are all expressed through whole body movements that we associate with those feelings and that story.

Pupils should be able to show that they can:

a *work safely, sensibly, co-operatively and unselfishly as members of a team.* By waiting nearly four years before including a dance expressing extreme aggression, it is hoped that the top year class will respond in a completely safe and sensible way to the instruction 'Never touch anyone!'

Lesson Plan – 30 minutes

Theme:
Traditional folk dance.

WARM-UP ACTIVITIES - 5 minutes

Music   Lively Caribbean style, carnival or steel band music.

1 The music is quite slow and your main body movement to start with is a lifting and lowering of each foot, keeping a flat 'lift and place' action going. 'One . . . . and two; lift . . . . and place.' The slowness of this action is made possible by a generous knee lift. 'Lift, then step; lift, then place; one . . . . and two.'

2 Steps are done almost on the spot with little transfer forwards of weight. All practise this one step forwards per bar of music into a circle for eight; then backwards out for eight.

3 Repeat to centre with loose, free swings of the upper body and shoulders, with gestures to contrast with the simple little movements of the feet. Eight in to centre and eight back out again.

4 With feet still for four counts, bounce your knees, but with a generous lifting, lowering, and swinging of arms and shoulders. Travel forwards for four; do four on the spot; four backwards; and four on the spot.

MOVEMENT SKILLS TRAINING - 15 minutes

1 Do two steps to each bar of music. Step forwards on to flat right foot and put your weight on it. Bring the ball of your left foot up beside your right foot, but keep weight on right foot. Step forwards on to flat left foot and put your weight on it. Bring the ball of your right foot up beside your left, but keep weight on left foot. Step forwards on to right foot. Step, close; and step, close; and step, close, all into circle for eight and backwards out for eight.

2 Try one slow, followed by two quick. Step left . . . . right, left; right . . . . left, right; 1 . . . . 2, 3; 1 . . . . 2, 3; slow . . . . quick, quick with one long and two short steps.

3 Show a partner your one or two patterns as you 'Follow the leader'. Let the upper body and arms work loosely and with big gestures since the feet are doing such simple movements.

4 You can be still for your start, simply letting upper body, arms and shoulders work loosely with little knee bounces, keeping the rhythm. Bounce . . . . and bounce; loose arms and shoulders; bounce and bounce; now travel . . . . and travel; one . . . . and two.

1 All follow me, keeping our big circle shape. It's important to keep following the person in front of you, as I lead you into a smaller and smaller circle, and then lead you out again. Go! (Teacher leads them round in the big starting circle, using the Caribbean steps already practised. The teacher goes inside those ahead of him or her to start a series of smaller circles. When the teacher runs out of space at the centre of the many concentric circles, he or she turns to go in the opposite direction, unwinding the many circles and re-creating the original circle. Clockwise into the maze is followed by anti-clockwise out from the maze.)

2 Well done. We got there. Now, in smaller circles of about eight dancers, let me see you making and unravelling your mazes.

LESSON NOTES AND NC GUIDANCE

Pupils should be taught to:

a *be physically active.*

b *adopt the best possible posture and use of the body.* In actions with little travelling and a great deal of movement within the body, we focus as much on what the whole body is doing as on what the legs are doing. Upper body, shoulders and arms, swinging, lifting and turning, give the dance a lively physicality that compensates for the quiet leg actions.

c *respond to music.*

d *perform a number of dances from different times and places.* In the same way that the 'Dashing White Sergeant' music and dance give an excellent insight into the typical folk music and dance of Scotland, this music and dance express the less vigorous, more gesture-filled style of the Caribbean. The cold Scottish winters require a lively, vigorous dance, performed indoors. The warmer West Indies favour an outdoor, relaxed, carnival style.

Pupils should be able to show that they can:

a *repeat a series of movements performed previously.* A repetitive pattern and rhythm are the main aids to practising, remembering, and being able to repeat sequences of movement. The smaller circles of the final part of the lesson will need to discuss, plan and agree the number of parts to their pattern, and decide how often to repeat each one.

Lesson Plan – 30 minutes

Theme:
Responding to music.

WARM-UP ACTIVITIES - 5 minutes

1 All crouch down in our large circle, bouncing on the spot.

2 Slowly rise up to standing and, on the spot, do easy steps and swings of free leg across standing leg.

3 Still facing the centre, do a side to side travel with a side, together, chasse action and handclaps each time your feet come together. Do four side to side chasse to each side.

4 All travel into the centre and out again, tall with a good 'swagger' of upper body from side to side.

5 Half of class go into circle and out, while the other half go out backwards and in again. (Ask class to suggest contrasting actions for the back and forwards travels.)

6 Travel round in a circle, to right and to left, four steps each way.

MOVEMENT SKILLS TRAINING - 15 minutes

1 In your groups of four, travel to your agreed places for your own choice of activities. Decide your group shape – two facing two; all in a line; in a circle; staying on the spot; travelling all together; or one, then two, and so on; circling round, hands joined; wheeling round and back, one hand in, making a star.

2 Decide the footwork to be used, often the step-swing across.

3 Throughout, the travelling is slow, 'easy', and unhurried, often with an accompanying handclap or a bounce of the upper body.

Music   From *The Best Of Glenn Miller*   (3 mins 27 secs).

1 From your separate groups, return, now, to the whole class circle, facing the centre, and stepping to right and to left, with handclaps.

2 On the spot, place one elbow in the other hand. The wrist of the high, held hand rotates to right and to left.

3 Strong step-swings with opposite arm and leg swinging across.

4 Crouch, bouncing, slowly rising up to finish with a high spring and gesture of the arms at the end, 'Yeah!'

5 Brilliant. Now, let's dance it all the way through, starting in our big circle, crouching down.

Time

0 secs   In a big circle, crouched, bouncing on the spot.

10 secs   Slow rise to standing.

15 secs   Easy steps with free leg swinging across standing leg.

28 secs   Side to side travel, facing centre, four chasse each way.

43 secs   All into centre and out again, with swagger of upper body.

56 secs   Half into circle and half out; then back to circle again.

1 min 6 secs   Travel in a circle, right and left, 4 counts each way.

1 min 36 secs   Own choices of group activities in groups of four.

2 mins 22 secs All return to whole class circle, stepping right and left, with handclaps.

2 mins 40 secs On the spot, one elbow in the other hand, rotating.

3 mins 0 secs   Step-swings with opposite arm and leg swings across.

3 mins 15 secs Crouch, bouncing, rising to high spring and 'Yeah!'

LESSON NOTES AND NC GUIDANCE

Pupils should be taught to:

a *respond to music.* Pupils will be interested to learn that this is probably the best-known piece of big band music from the era of big bands and ballroom dancing after the last war. In 'responding' to more than three minutes of music, it helps to have a start directed by the teacher, a middle planned by the groups, and an ending directed by the teacher

b *compose and control their movements by varying shape, size, level, direction, speed and tension.* The groups of four will be asked to decide their group shape; actions and any travelling directions; and whether they will move with small, soft steps, big, swinging, strong leg and arm movements, or a mixture of the two.

Pupils should be able to show that they can:

a *respond imaginatively to the various challenges.* The middle of the dance provides nearly one minute of pupil-centred, imaginative responding. For variety, the teacher might encourage different group alignments – a line, circle, square, wheel – but the content will be the result of group planning and group decision-making.

Pupil response might include jiving by those who have attended Dance classes out of school.

Lesson Plan – 30 minutes

Theme:
Responding imaginatively to music as members of a team.

WARM-UP ACTIVITIES - 5 minutes

1 Walk round freely, by yourself, to this well known, slow, Rock Around The Clock music by Bill Haley. Take one step to each count of the music. Feel the rhythm, feel the rhythm, 1, 2, 3, 4; step and step, 1, 2, 3, 4.

2 Because the stepping is slow, you have plenty of time to add in big arm and shoulder swings from side to side. Please add something to make your simple travelling look more interesting.

3 All face the front, feet still, doing big arm swings from side to side. Do four swings standing; four with a bending of the knees; four with a stretching of the knees; and four, standing. Let your upper body and arm movements liven up an otherwise quiet action.

4 After that rest for your legs, do eight lively hop swings where you step on to a foot, then hop and swing the opposite leg across the hopping one. Do eight to the right and eight to the left with vigour! Hop-swing; hop-swing; lively, lively; 5, 6, 7, keep going.

5 Well done, lively dancers. Walk again for eight counts, with free leg and opposite arm swinging straight forwards, then turn and do eight back again. Step, swing; step, reach; 3, 4, 5, 6, 7, turn.

MOVEMENT SKILLS TRAINING - 10 minutes

1 In your groups of four, join hands with well bent arms to make a small circle. Step to left, then close right to left, in a slow chasse. Each chasse takes two counts of the music. Do five chasse in each direction. Chasse left, chasse left, 3, 4, now right.

2 Fours divide into two pairs who link right arms to do eight running steps to left, then to right with left arms linked. Your free arm is held high as you wave to the others. Go!

3 Well done. Now, let me talk you through our developing 'Rock 'n' Roll' dance, as we practised from the start of the lesson. All stand, well spaced round the room for your walk to group lines starting places. Ready? Keep listening to my reminders. Walking . . . . go! Into lines now, facing front.

4 Four arm swings, standing . . . . knees bending . . . . knees stretching . . . . standing . . . . eight hop swings to right.

5 Hop, swing, hop swing, 3, 4, 5, 6, 7, to left; hop swing, lively, 3, 4, 5, 6, 7, now walk right.

6 Walk, 2, 3, 4, 5, 6, 7, turn; walk back, 3, 4, 5, 6, make your circle.

7 Chasse left, 2, 3, 4, 5; chasse right, 2, 3, link arm with partner.

8 Quick running, elbows linked, 5, 6, 7, turn; quick running, wave other arm, 5, 6, 7, well done.

Music   *Rock Around The Clock* by Bill Haley (2 mins 6 secs).

1 In the middle of the dance, there are 30 seconds when your group of four will use imagination, please, and plan your very own actions. Decide your actions first. You can work together in a line; or moving, two by two, from your line; or in a rippling action down the line; or have pairs meeting and passing, under an arch; or one can perform on the spot with the others circling round.

2 For variety and contrast can you include at least two group actions? Maybe one on the spot and one moving; or one in line and one with pairs facing; or one that is 'easy' and one that is lively and vigorous. Keep discussing and practising, please.

3 Well done. You all seem to have agreed, practised and remembered your own, newly created, group activity.

4 To finish the dance, there will be 36 seconds, during which all do the same movement, as at the start of the dance. All stand facing the same way, behind a leader. Put both hands on the shoulders of the person in front of you.

5 To avoid kicking the person in front of you, the action is done with feet apart, hopping on each foot in turn, and turning your head to look out to the side of your hopping leg. The forwards travel on each bouncy hop is short. Let's try it, starting on the right foot. Go! Hop, and, hop, and, right, and left; small step, small step, bounce and bounce; together, together, 1 and 2.

Good. That looked very neat and together.

6 Go to your well-spaced starting positions and we will try the whole dance through, from the beginning, with me reminding you of the order of actions.

Time

0 secs   With the music, start your walk to places in lines of four.

10 secs   Face front, arm swings, standing; knees bending, knees stretching, standing.

20 secs   Hop swings to left, for 3, for 4; arm and leg swings, for 3 and turn; hop swings to right for 3, for 4; arm and leg swings for 3, now walk.

30 secs   Walk to right, arm swings, 3, 4, 5, 6, 7, turn; walk to left, walk left, swing the arms, 5, 6, 7, into circle.

40 secs   Slow chasse; step, close; left, close; 4 and 5, turn; slow chasse; step, close; right, close; 4 and partners.

50 secs   Quick running, elbows joined, 5, 6, 7, turn; quick running, wave your arm, 5, 6, 7, now your group actions.

1 min   Own choices of group sequences.

1 min 30 secs   Bouncing lines, bouncing, bouncing; into a big circle, anti-clockwise round.

1 min 55 secs   Still in your circle, face the centre, holding partner with one hand while other hand waves to classmates.

2 mins 6 secs   Music and dance end.

LESSON NOTES AND NC GUIDANCE

Pupils should be able to show that they can:

a plan to respond imaginatively to challenges. To make the pupils' imaginative responses manageable, the teacher directs the start and the finish, and challenges the groups of four pupils to plan the middle of their dance.

b *practise, improve and refine performance, and repeat a series of movements with increasing control and accuracy.* We also want an enthusiastic, stylish and poised performance that is obviously being enjoyed enormously.

c *make simple judgements about their own and others' performances and use this information to improve the quality.* Appreciative, encouraging evaluation enhances the pleasure experienced when giving a performance.

Useful Addresses

The English Folk Dance and Song Society
Dance books and music: Cecil Sharp House, 2 Regents Park Road, London NW1 7AY (tel. 0207 485 2206).

The Society For International Folk Dancing
Membership Secretary: Alan Morton, 26 Durham Road, Harrow HA1 4PG (tel. 0208 427 8042) www.sifd.org
Dance books and music: Eleanor Gordon, 92 Norbiton Avenue, Kingston upon Thames, Surrey KT1 3QP.
Other enquiries: Jeanette Hull, Secretary, 24 The Homeland, London Road, Mordon, Surrey SM4 5AS. A list of general and specialist classes is obtainable from the membership secretary. Society members are available to visit schools, clubs and classes to teach a selection of dances.

National Youth Jazz Orchestra (NYJO)
Superb, modern, rhythmic music which never becomes dated, because it is written specially for the orchestra. Music is particularly good for warm-ups. Slow for big body movements, turning and gestures; medium for bouncy stepping and travelling; fast for speedier skipping and travelling.
Director: Bill Ashton, 11 Victor Road, Harrow, Middlesex HA2 6PT.
Tel: 0181 863 8685 for music list and order forms, or visit the website at www.nyjo.org.uk

The Royal Scottish Country Dance Society
Contact: The Secretary, 12 Coates Crescent, Edinburgh EH3 7AF for information on publications and videos.
Tel: 0131 225 3854
web address: www.scottishdance.org

Index